I0535032

Published by Samantha Sabian and Arianthem Press

THE DRAGON'S WAR Vol 7 CHRONICLES OF ARIANTHEM, 2015. FIRST PRINTING.

Office of Publication: Los Angeles, California

THE DRAGON'S WAR, CHRONICLES OF ARIANTHEM, its logo, all related characters and their likenesses are ™ and © and ™ 2015 Samantha Sabian and Arianthem Press.

ALL RIGHTS RESERVED. The entire contents of this book are © 2015 Samantha Sabian. Any similarities to persons living or dead are purely coincidental. With the exception of artwork used for review purposes, none of the contents of this book may be reprinted in any form without the express written consent of Samantha Sabian.

What did you think of this book? We love to hear from our readers.

Please email us at: samantha@arianthem.com.

THE DRAGON'S WAR

THE CHRONICLES OF ARIANTHEM VII

SAMANTHA SABIAN

ARIANTHEM PRESS

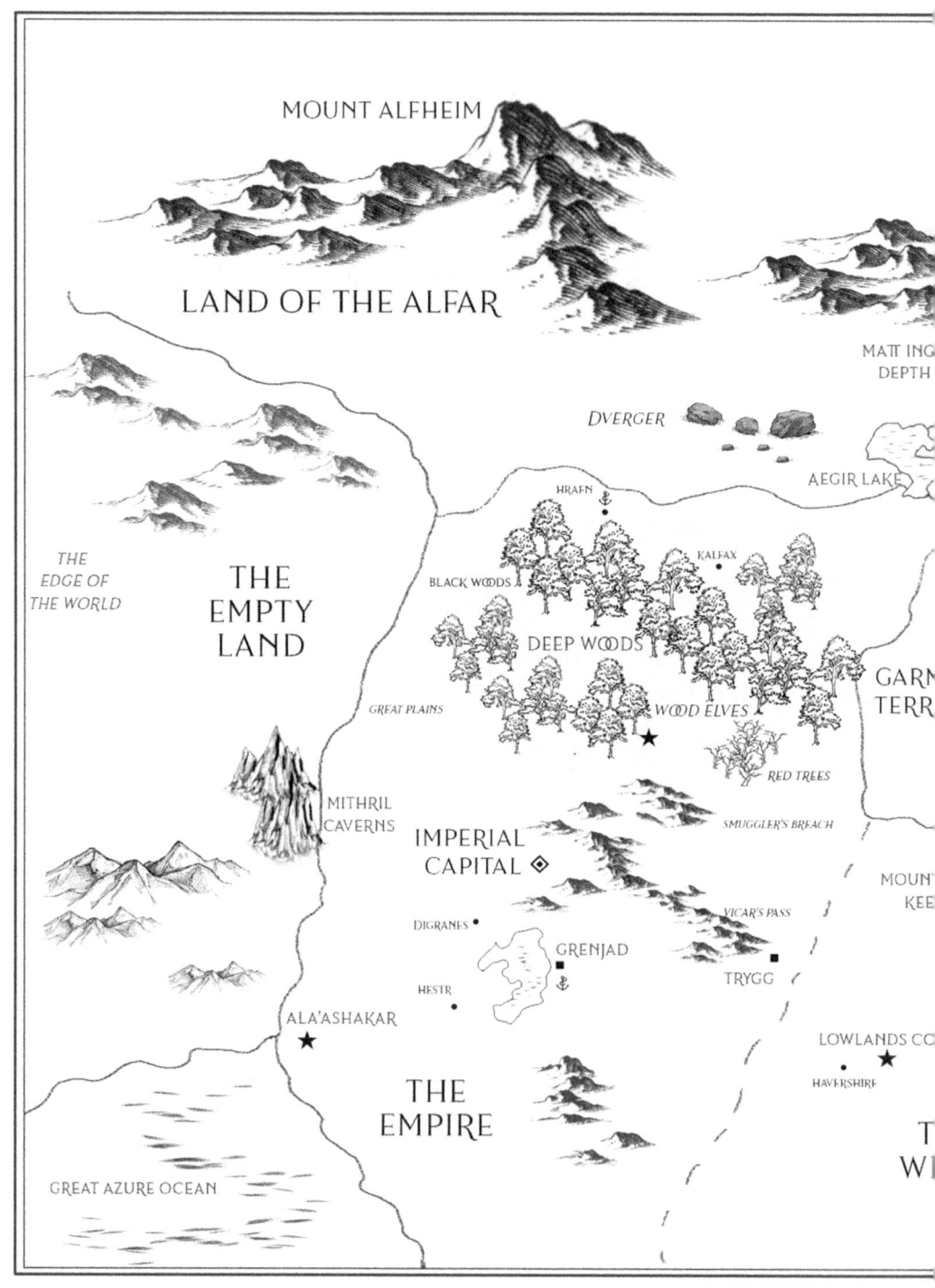

AGONS

KYLAN'S
CASTLE
★

BALDUR'S PEAK

DARBY FALLS
REIST KEEP

DVERGER

NTER
ITORY

GUDRID

HALDIS◈

THE
SJOFN ACADEMY
★

LAND OF THE
HA'KAN

ARIANTHEM
CIRCA 312 AGW

CHAPTER 1

The women standing at the top of the steps of the Ha'kan palace were all similar, yet a study in contrast. Their similarity was an uncommon size and beauty; their dissimilarity was the way in which that beauty was manifested. Astrid, the High Priestess of the Ha'kan, the woman responsible for the ultimate sexual well-being of her people, was a vision of elegant and sensual grace, the robes of her vocation hugging the curves of her body. Gimle, the First Scholar, the head of the Scholar's caste, was slender and lovely, her scholar's robes giving hint to the mysteries that lie beneath. Senta, the First General, was the largest in height and size, her gleaming armor adding to her size, her handsome features and confident demeanor adding to her allure.

And then there was the Queen. Halla was resplendent in her royal robes, a perfect mixture of the castes of her society, possessing the sensuality of a priestess, the wisdom of a scholar, and the strength of a warrior. She was both the leader and epitome of the Ha'kan, the all-female race that rivaled the empire in military might and influence. And today she waited with great expectation and a trace of unease for the return of those dearest to her.

"I think I see them," Senta commented, shielding her eyes. "The Tavinter scouts said they were close."

Halla's heart gave a little flutter as she, too, saw the dust from the horses. Her daughter was more than capable on her own, a fearless warrior and a respected military leader. Still, it had been difficult to let her go, even though she was accompanied by the Tavinter and her own future First General. Rika was growing as formidable as her mentor and she would lay down her life for Dallan without hesitation.

The clatter of hoofbeats on the cobblestone streets of the Ha'kan capital grew louder and many cheered as the Princess and her entourage passed at breathtaking speed. It had been a long journey, but the horses sensed their riders' enthusiasm and rallied for the last stretch. They flew across the bridge to the castle and entered the courtyard where the panting beasts were corralled by the royal ostlers. Dallan tossed the reins to the nearest as she slid from the horse's back, patting his twitching flanks in appreciation. Rika, too, dismounted, a huge grin on her face. It was good to be home.

One fair-haired rider sat on her horse, glancing about her with a bemused expression on her face. This felt very familiar, but in an odd way. It was as if the world about her were blurry and slowly returning to focus. Or rather it was not the world that was blurry, but her memories of it, which were slowly gaining in clarity. She slid to the ground as she was greeted enthusiastically by all near.

"Are you okay, Skye?" Torsten asked. He was Tavinter, like Skye, and her second-in-command. He had also been her friend since childhood.

"Yes," Skye said with growing certainty. "I'm fine."

"Then let me take your horse, the Queen will want to see you."

Dallan stood at the base of the stairs. "Torsten's right, Skye. My mother will want to see you. Come now."

Skye continued to glance around as she joined Dallan and Rika and started up the steps, and more things came into focus. This was the Ha'kan capital where she lived. Her quarters would be in Dallan's chambers, the circular area where the future Royal Staff lived, the one that was opposite and adjacent to the Queen's chambers. This thought brought her wandering eyes to the terrace above, the one where four gorgeous women stood. Her musings had slowed her pace and Dallan and Rika were already at the top of the steps, showered with embraces and motherly assessments of their well-being. She slowed even further, and the last step was taken almost tentatively as she stood examining the four before her one-by-one. She smiled shyly, for she remembered them all.

"Your Majesty," Skye said, then bowed in the formal Tavinter custom.

"Oh, Skye," Halla said, abandoning all royal protocol. She stepped forward and clutched the young woman to her breast, causing Skye all sorts of pleasant consternation and profuse blushing. And the fact that the Queen held her for so long, perhaps even longer than she had held her daughter, caused Dallan to grin. Skye did not speak of it, but she had long had a crush on the entire Royal Staff, and Dallan was pleased to see she remembered it.

Halla released her, but Skye was only briefly free as Astrid enveloped her in another, not-quite-maternal embrace that, if possible, made her blush even more. The Queen and High Priestess had occupied her dreams for years, and right now, she could remember the fantasies more than the realities. The sensuality of the two together was overwhelming.

And then there was Senta, a different kind of overwhelming, but one no less powerful. The stern general looked gently down on her young charge, and a flood of memories returned to Skye. Of Senta at the Academy, kissing the First General mischievously on a training exercise, of the First General waiting years to repay that playful action. Skye's fantasies of the First General were just as vivid as those of the Queen and Astrid, the only difference being that many of them had come true.

"First General," Skye said formally.

Senta placed her hands on Skye's shoulders, examining the little Tavinter beauty who was so different from the Ha'kan. Although the Ha'kan varied widely in features, they tended towards darker hair and fair skin. Skye's olive skin, her fair hair, and hazel eyes were exotic to the once-secluded people, and they had welcomed her as they had few others.

"First Ranger," Senta said, just as formally.

Skye cocked her head to the side, and Senta continued. "That's the title we decided upon in your absence."

The corner of Skye's mouth curled upward, creating the slightest dimple in her cheek, and Senta could remain formal no longer. She pulled the young woman to her and hugged her tightly. Skye could barely breathe, but it felt so wonderful and safe to be held by the First General.

"Oh great," Rika muttered, "that means she outranks us both."

Dallan chuckled, for strictly speaking, that was true. Skye had attended the Academy with them as part of an innovative exchange program and had always been a part of Dallan's cohort and her staff. But in theory, Dallan was the future Queen and Rika was the future First General, whereas Skye was now the current First Ranger. Not that Skye would lord it over them, for she was unassuming to a fault and preferred the company of the younger Ha'kan. The younger were playfully sexual, but the elder Ha'kan possessed a sensuality that was monumentally distracting.

"That means you'll be earth far more than you're used to," Dallan teased, for the Ha'kan used the terms "earth" and "sky" to refer to how dominant a woman was in bed.

"Fine by me," Rika said, "I've missed her so."

This caused a cloud to pass over Dallan's features. She, too, longed for Skye with a passion that was nearly uncontrollable. The Ha'kan did not value monogamy and serial sexual partners were not only the norm but expected, for sex was a soothing, pleasurable experience that permeated the fabric of their society. Skill in the bedroom was as crucial for success as any other skill within Ha'kan culture. Friendships, contracts, and alliances were formed in bed, and even conflicts were resolved through sexual interaction. Love did not always accompany sex, but sex always accompanied love, and Dallan loved Skye dearly.

But Dallan had not approached Skye since her rescue, nor had Rika. Their return had been pell-mell, a headlong race through imperial territory in their haste to get home. They had hardly rested the entire journey, and most in the troupe fell into an exhausted sleep the minute they stopped. She had held Skye as she slept, as had Rika, but neither had done more than kissed her.

Dallan's expression darkened. She had to admit that was not the whole reason for her hesitation. They had been in a band of soldiers and rangers, and there had been little opportunity to speak with Skye alone. Dallan did not know what had happened to Skye, what the sorceress had done to her in her captivity. She did know that Skye's memory had been taken from her and she had lived with her enemy for months as her lover. But Skye had said little on the way home and had been lost in thought, a perplexed and faraway look in her eye.

There was no such look in her eye as the First General released Skye and she moved on to the First Scholar. Lately, Skye's memories would return with such rapidity it would make her head hurt, but right now, the memories brought her nothing but pleasure. Gimle took Skye's hands in her own as the young woman spoke.

"You saved us all, you know."

"And how did I do that?" the willowy scholar asked, her cool refinement as beguiling as Astrid's heated elegance.

"Just when all seemed lost, I remembered our lesson on the invisibility spell and was able to use it."

Gimle smiled as she recalled the lesson as well. She had taken the young woman to her bed and forbidden her to touch her until she turned herself invisible. Skye was able to do so and remained in that state for an extended period of time, during which she was allowed to do anything she wanted, and the First Scholar had benefited from her comprehensive exploration.

"Once you're settled, we'll have to renew your lessons," Gimle said, releasing her.

"I'd like that," Skye said happily, and all Ha'kan breathed a quiet sigh of relief, for that was a wonderful sign. It was also an opportunity for Astrid to segue into the next reunion.

"Speaking of which," the High Priestess said, "there's one who has anxiously awaited your return."

Skye turned at Astrid's gesture and saw an exquisite young woman standing at the edge of the terrace. She was radiant, exuding warmth and love, and she gazed at Skye expectantly.

"Lifa," Skye breathed out, and moved to her. Her eyes traveled over the beloved features, the full lips, the lovely cheek bones, the auburn hair. Lifa took her hands and engaged in her own examination, but one far more penetrating. Although her eyes lingered on Skye's lips, they focused most intently on those hazel eyes, weighing, assessing, determining. And based upon what she saw, the future High Priestess of the Ha'kan leaned forward and kissed Skye fully on the mouth, deeply, passionately, withholding nothing. And Skye returned the kiss, also without restraint.

At last, Lifa drew back, took Skye by the hand, and led her from the terrace.

"Let us go walk in the garden."

Astrid watched her future successor leave with pride. It was appropriate that Lifa be the one to assess Skye's well-being and ease the transition of her return. Lifa would not have pressed Skye in any way had she sensed unease, but Skye's ardent response indicated Lifa had judged her mood well. And the fact that Skye had left the terrace under Lifa's spell without a backward glance was an excellent sign. The Queen expressed Astrid's thoughts aloud.

"Thank the Divine," Halla said, sighing. She turned to her daughter. "I was so worried what that sorceress might have done to her."

"I'm not sure what happened," Dallan said, "we didn't really have the chance to talk about it yet. I'm hoping Lifa can work her magic."

"I should have sent a Priestess with you," Astrid said, a trace of self-recrimination in her voice, "there are many who are trained for battlefield situations."

"If Skye were Ha'kan," Rika said, "I think she would be fine. From what Syn said, it sounded like the sorceress convinced her they were lovers. Unlike before, I don't think she was forced or tortured."

"And from what I remember of her from her visit to the Academy," Gimle murmured, "I'm sure the sorceress is excellent in bed."

"Agreed," Rika said. "If it were me, I'd be angry at the lies and abduction when my memory returned, but everything before that really wouldn't have bothered me."

"Well," the Queen said, "let's hope Skye will take this like a Ha'kan."

Lifa and Skye walked hand-in-hand through the royal garden. There were a few women about enjoying the fresh air and flowers, and they enjoyed the sight of the future High Priestess and lovely little Tavinter even more. Lifa waved greetings to them as they passed, but Skye saw only Lifa.

"Thank you," Skye said shyly.

"For what?" Lifa asked, swinging Skye's hand.

"For kissing me like that. I've felt like I'm contaminated or something with Dallan and Rika jumping around me."

Lifa stopped abruptly and pulled Skye to her, wrapping her hands about her waist and pressing her full body against her. The feel of Lifa's breasts against her was wonderful and Skye's eyes went to the cleavage that had deepened upon the contact. When she looked up, Lifa again kissed her, a lengthy, searing kiss that took Skye's breath away. Lifa pressed her forehead to Skye's forehead.

"I can tell by the look on their faces they don't think you contaminated. Dallan looks like she's in agony."

"Really?"

"Oh yes," Lifa said, "and the only reason they've hesitated is to make sure you're all right."

"Why wouldn't I be all right?" Skye asked, her brow furrowing.

"You have no idea how good it is to hear you say that," Lifa said, laughing. She took Skye's hand and they began walking again.

"None of us really knows what happened with you and the sorceress. The last time she took you, she hurt you."

Skye paled a little. She had forgotten all about that and Lifa wished she had not reminded her. But Skye pushed the memory away.

"It wasn't like that this time. I woke up months ago without knowing where or who I was. Eydis, or rather Ingrid, told me we were lovers and I had nothing to convince me otherwise. At first, she was actually kind to me, although a little possessive."

"And later?" Lifa asked carefully.

Skye was thoughtful. "In the beginning, she convinced me I was a delicate little flower that had fallen off a horse and hit my head."

Lifa muffled laughter, for she could think of nothing so out-of-character for Skye.

"I think she did that on purpose," Skye said, "giving me a background so at odds with my real self. There was nothing to trigger any memories. But later, I killed a Hell Hound that wandered into the fields, and I think she realized my mind was beginning to return."

"And then what happened?" Lifa asked, watching Skye closely.

Skye had a faraway look in her eye, reassessing events she had lived through under a haze. It was difficult to analyze them, to chronicle them in a coherent order. Eydis had changed, become harder, more watchful, gradually dropping the charade as parts of Skye returned. But that hadn't been all bad.

Lifa saw the mischievous look on Skye's face, the twinkle in her eye she adored.

"What?"

"There was a time when my memory first began to return, and the sorceress also began to act like herself, but I still didn't know who she was. I just thought that 'Eydis' had begun to act strange."

"And?"

"It was very—," Skye said, then paused. "Enjoyable."

"Ah," Lifa said. "Angry sex can be very passionate."

"Yes," Skye agreed. "Yes, it can."

Lifa stopped before a door, and Skye was surprised to find they had walked all the way through the garden and were now at the tiered entry to the Royal Staff quarters occupied by the younger Ha'kan. She glanced to the doors along the circular structure. If she remembered correctly, her chambers were over there. The door they stood in front of bore the symbols of the Priestess caste.

"Would you like to join me in my chambers?"

Skye's shy smile returned. "You so rarely stay in your own room. You're not going to the Ministry?"

"If you wish, we could go there. But I thought you might enjoy a bath after your journey."

Skye's eyes lit up at the thought, and Lifa took her hand. "Come along now."

Lifa's chambers were exactly as Skye remembered them, and she catalogued the contents as each memory took hold. The tiled bath, gently sloped and easily large enough for two, was full of soapy water that carried hints of lavender on tendrils of steam that drifted upward. Leya and Freya, two of Lifa's inner circle, were present. The Priestesses greeted Skye warmly, but quickly dismissed themselves, leaving Skye and Lifa alone.

"Now, off with those dusty clothes."

Skye had often marveled at the Ha'kan skill in disrobing women, and none could rival the skill of the Priestess caste, let alone the future High Priestess. As if by magic, her shirt was over her head, her boots set aside, and her pants dropped to the floor. The undergarments were whisked away, and she stood naked on the warm tile floor.

Lifa's appreciation showed in her eyes. If Skye had spent the last few months in a pampered existence, it certainly didn't show. She was as lean and muscled as ever, and if anything, a trifle thin. Lifa took her by the hand.

"Come now, into the bath."

Skye stepped down into the marble pool. The hot water was luxurious and Skye settled in up to her waist. Although she had taken many enjoyable baths in captivity, there was nothing quite like the beauty and safety of the Ha'kan palace.

And then there was Lifa, who was now disrobing, an action that absorbed all Skye's attention. It did not seem possible, but Lifa was even more beautiful than she remembered. Her breasts were fuller, her skin was radiant, and she glowed with the inner light that had always illuminated her and everyone around her. But now that light was brighter than the sun. She slipped in behind Skye, reaching for the scented soap, pressing her breasts against Skye's back as she did so.

Skye relaxed against Lifa as the High Priestess spread lather over her body. Although Lifa's actions were not overtly sexual, they were so casually sensual they had an even more pronounced effect. The ministrations were both tender and gentle, yet even the most hardened Ha'kan warrior freely admitted that the Priestess caste were the most dominant members of their society. Skye could not help herself and turned to kiss Lifa, a bruising, longing kiss filled with desperation. And Lifa returned the kiss, her passion igniting. The breasts pressed hard against the muscular back and one lathered hand went to a firm breast while the other dipped beneath the water to work its magic. Skye twisted and turned beneath the skilled hands while Lifa held her tight, still stealing her breath with a kiss. It was not long before Skye's body released, never breaking the kiss of her lover.

Lifa at last released Skye from the bondage of that kiss and leaned back, Skye still comfortably in her arms. The two rested for a while, Lifa still languorously washing Skye, when Skye turned to Lifa with an impish look in her eye.

"Are you tired?"

"Of course not," Lifa replied. "Did you forget the stamina required of a Priestess?"

"I could never forget that," Skye said, "which is why I'd like to move to the bed. I could never hold my breath long enough to do what I want to do here, and your stamina would surely cause me to drown."

Lifa laughed and took her by the hand. "Then by all means, let us move. I don't want to be the cause of your demise."

They both took up soft towels, drying the other, and that act alone was enough to send them back into another embrace. They made it to the bed, the soft, lovely haven large enough for several participants, and collapsed into the deep cushions. Skye was on top and began kissing Lifa everywhere, her eyes, her lips her throat, her breasts, her stomach, and finally down to the softness between her legs where she settled for an extended length of time. And Lifa cradled that beloved head in her hands, marveling at the skill of those lips and that tongue, thinking for the thousandth time what an excellent Priestess Skye would have made had she chosen that vocation. When her body released, it was with an abandon the High Priestess exhibited with few.

Skye pushed Lifa until she was certain she was fully satisfied, then pulled herself up next to her and lie with her head upon her shoulder. Lifa toyed with her hair, kissing the fair strands still damp from the bath. Sometimes Skye would doze off in the gentle afterglow, but today, although feeling a pleasant lethargy, she was nowhere near sleep.

Lifa sensed this, and quietly took advantage of the opportunity.

"You've returned at a perfect time. I'm still responsible for your sexual development, and very soon you'll have to learn something new."

Skye raised her head, concerned. "Do you find me wanting?"

Lifa's laughter bubbled over. "By the gods, no. Tell me you're more aware than that."

"Well, yes. I just wanted to make sure."

"No, this is something entirely new that you just haven't had the chance to experience."

Now Skye was very curious. Her time with the Ha'kan had been a non-stop cornucopia of sexual experience, so she couldn't imagine what she had missed.

"You're going to have to learn how to safely make love to a pregnant woman," Lifa said.

Skye felt a surge of excitement. This was a boundless honor. Pregnancy was a rare and revered event in Ha'kan culture. Despite their advanced medical and scientific knowledge, no one was quite certain how reproduction occurred. It was entirely independent of sex and rested solely with the mother through parthenogenesis. This quirk of evolution greatly shaped their culture and society, leading many scholars to propose that their sexual freedom was a direct result of this unique procreation, for neither the reproductive process nor the overt sexuality existed in any other race in Arianthem.

Although pregnancy was to some extent rare, Ha'kan children were fiercely protected and few were ever lost. Most women had only one or two children, but some were prolific and had several. The race was long-lived and dominant in battle, and with all these factors together, the population continued to gradually grow.

"That's wonderful!" Skye exclaimed. "Who will be—"

Skye stopped, for Lifa was looking at her expectantly. Skye's eyes drifted down to where Lifa rested her hand on her still-flat stomach.

"You?" Skye said with wonder. "You're with child?"

"I am," Lifa said proudly, and Skye now understood Lifa's newly acquired luminance.

Skye fairly pounced on her, hugging her tightly, then drew back, concerned.

"Did I hurt you? I'm so sorry."

"And this will be lesson number one," Lifa said. "You may not treat me like a porcelain doll. Ha'kan women are very resilient when pregnant."

Skye grinned. "I'm sure they are."

A quiet knock on the door somehow communicated a circumspect intensity.

"I'm guessing that Astrid has told the others. Come in," she said, slightly louder.

Dallan and Rika strode in, having themselves cleaned and changed clothes. They could hardly contain their joy, rushing to the bed.

"Is it true?" Dallan asked.

"It is," Lifa said, the pride still in her voice.

Dallan fairly lifted Lifa from the bed, hugging her tightly. Rika then took her turn at nearly squeezing Lifa to death, then set her gently back down on the pile of pillows. Dallan sat down next to her, and Rika sprawled at the foot of the bed. Lifa took Skye back into her arms and pulled the sheet up around them, not out of modesty but because there was a slight chill in the air.

"I was just telling Skye she would have a new opportunity for development."

Rika grinned. "That's right. She's not had the pleasure, yet."

"You have?" Skye asked.

"Of course," Rika said, "we learned the theory of it our third year at the Academy."

"You learned more than theory," Dallan reminded her.

"Ah, that's right," Rika said, relishing the memory. "As did you."

"Why am I not surprised?" Skye said. Both Dallan and Rika were so charming, even at a young age, it was likely they received far more "training" than the average Ha'kan.

Lifa ran her fingers through Skye's hair. Once again, the Tavinter did not recognize that her own charm put her on level with both the Princess and future First General, and the only reason she had not yet received the training was the numerous absences that fate had brought her way.

"You're in for a treat," Rika said.

"What do you mean?" Skye asked. She had thought the training would revolve around making certain the pregnant woman was comfortable and the child uninjured.

Both Dallan and Rika deferred to Lifa on the subject.

"The sexual drive of the Ha'kan woman peaks at two times during her life," Lifa explained. "One is when she reaches her fourth or fifth decade, and then that lasts for a very long time. The second is when she's with child."

"Really?" Skye asked, her eyes wide.

"Yes," Lifa said, "we can be insatiable."

"I can't imagine," Skye said, mulling over this seemingly impossible fact.

"Kara is already hovering about me," Lifa said to Dallan. "She's determined to assist with every birth in the capital to prepare for mine."

"That sounds like her."

"She wanted to be here for your return, but there's a woman giving birth in the market quarter, so she's with the midwife and those closest to the mother."

This caused another little tug of a grin on Dallan's face.

"What?" Skye asked.

"It's one more good reason why you've returned to us now."

"It's widely believed," Lifa explained, "that the child bonds to the mother's lovers while still in the womb. That the strength of that bond is a direct result of the sexual intensity between the mother and lovers during pregnancy."

"Oh," Skye said slowly. That explained a lot. No wonder Astrid, Gimle, and Senta were as much Dallan's parents as was the Queen. Ha'kan reproduction was so physically different from other races they did not have traditional families. But they had formed something just as strong, if not stronger. Rika had once revealed that her own mother, a trusted member of Senta's staff, had been killed when she was very young, but that the Queen had treated her just like a daughter.

"So," Dallan said, "my mother has ordered celebrations. Although the Ha'kan need little excuse to rejoice, Skye's safe return and the pregnancy of the future High Priestess are events worth celebrating. There'll be parties, contests, and guests from all over the country. And that will get you warmed up for an even bigger event."

"What's that?" Skye asked as Dallan removed an official looking scroll from inside her tunic. Dallan handed her the scroll. Skye unrolled the parchment and slowly read the graceful scrawl.

"This is an invitation to the Alfar Ceremony of Assumption," Skye said in wonder.

"You're the leader of the Tavinter," Dallan reminded her, "as well as First Ranger of the Ha'kan. It's only proper that you attend."

"Are all of you going?" Skye asked.

"No," Dallan said, shaking her head. "My mother will attend because it's her royal duty, and I must stay behind because it's mine."

There was a trace of disappointment in Dallan's voice, but it was eclipsed by her delight. "I get to run the country while my mother is gone."

"Really?" Skye asked, her eyes glowing at the thought. "And you'll be in charge of the military?" she asked, turning to Rika.

"I will," Rika said with pride. "Senta will leave behind her Second-in-Command, of course, just in case. But the forces will be mine in her absence."

"And Kara will head the Scholar's caste, and the Ministry will be mine," Lifa said. "The Queen thought this was a very good opportunity for us to 'practice,' if you will."

"And 'tis safest," Dallan commented, "just in case." Her countenance darkened at the thought. "Although I'm sure nothing will happen to my mother as long as Senta is with her."

"And don't forget Raine," Rika said, nudging her friend. "It's certain she'll be there, and there's no safer place than at her side."

"That's true," Dallan said, breathing a little easier. "And it's only for a fortnight."

"Perhaps I should stay," Skye said doubtfully. Both options sounded wonderful.

"You're a head of state," Dallan reminded her, "and a member of my mother's staff, so it's appropriate for you to go. Although I admit," Dallan said, ruffling her hair, "I wouldn't let you go if the trip were any longer. You just got back."

"That parting is still months off," Lifa said, "so let's enjoy our time together."

CHAPTER 2

T he Ha'kan capital was decorated in dazzling style with colorful stream-
ers, flowers, and banners. The castle courtyard glittered with red and
gold armor, pastel gowns, and lovely intricate robes as the communal society
came together as one. Skye walked around in a daze of disbelief, unable to
comprehend that a great deal of the celebration was for her. It reminded her
of the celebration at the Academy many years ago, when the girls' mothers
came to see their offspring, and of course, to see one another.

She came across a group of women who were a few years older than
Dallan and her cohort. All Ha'kan were beautiful, but this group was stunning. They all seemed to know one another and greeted each other with
enthusiastic hugs. Skye watched them curiously, for there was something
strangely familiar about all of them although she was certain they had never
met. Then Lifa came out, flowed toward them, and the greetings were even
more passionately enthusiastic. Skye had a sudden attack of shyness and
stepped back into the shadows, but Lifa caught sight of her movement.

"Oh, no you don't," she said, laughing, and went to capture the Tavinter.
She took Skye by the hand and led her to the group of smiling women.

"So, this is the one we've heard so much about."

The woman speaking was a statuesque Scholar, perhaps the largest one Skye had ever seen. Her brown eyes were intelligent and warm, framed with long dark eyelashes that set off splendid features.

"I'm honored to meet you," Skye said, bowing while her cheeks grew warm.

"Oh, she is adorable," said another, the emphasis leaving no doubt Skye had been a topic of conversation, although Skye was not certain with whom.

The woman speaking was a Priestess, possessing the provocative, sultry elegance that the truly gifted in the Ministry possessed. The woman next to her was a warrior but possessed a great deal of the same seductive manner. Skye wondered if they were related. The fourth of the foursome was also a warrior, slighter in frame, winsome, but just as magnetic as her three companions.

Then Dallan and Rika rushed into the courtyard and an explosion of greetings and happy reunions commenced, and Skye took the opportunity to take a step back to observe the curious scene. To her surprise, Dallan and Rika were joined by Gimle and Senta, then Astrid gracefully joined the mêlée of embraces. Finally, even the Queen herself arrived and joined the tumult.

"Who are these women?" Skye murmured to herself.

"You don't know?" Kara said, having slipped up beside her.

"No," Skye said, "they all look so familiar, but I'm sure I've never met them."

"There's a reason they look familiar," Kara said. "The tall scholar there, Runa, that's Senta's daughter."

"Senta has a daughter?" Skye exploded, then covered her mouth as Kara laughed. Skye was thankful the group of women was still so boisterous, otherwise they would have heard her outburst.

"Of course, she has a daughter."

"And her daughter is a scholar?" Skye asked in disbelief.

"Why not?" Kara asked, as if the question were nonsensical. "All Ha'kan are allowed to choose their professions, and unless completely unsuitable, that becomes their vocation. I've never really known anyone to be refused. The slender warrior there, that's Solvi, Gimle's daughter."

Skye stared in wonder at the lovely warrior in the embrace of the First Scholar, who did indeed look a great deal like her mother.

"And the other two?" Skye said, almost afraid to ask.

Kara gave her a wicked look. "You know who they are," she said over her shoulder as she went to join the greetings.

And indeed, Skye did know the two women as each hung on the arm of their mother, the High Priestess of the Ha'kan. Astrid kissed both of her beautiful daughters, showing no more favor to the priestess than she did the warrior, for both filled the vast space of her heart. And as the warrior daughter sent Skye a smoldering, knowing glance, Skye realized she probably took after her mother just as much as her sister, regardless of vocation.

Skye sighed, realizing there was still so much about Ha'kan culture that she didn't grasp. And although she had spent so many of the last few years with Dallan and her staff, she knew very little about their lives before the Academy. They had probably known these women most of their lives. She quietly left the inner courtyard.

Astrid watched her departure, as did her future successor. Lifa started to go after her when she felt a hand on her arm. Eira, Astrid's younger daughter had stayed her progress.

"Might I?" she asked.

"Of course," Lifa said, and her gratitude was genuine. "I'm sure she's heading for the archery range."

"Then I'll go keep her company."

Dallan had also watched Skye's departure with concern and was pleased to see Eira go after her. Eira was one of the best archers in the Ha'kan forces and would provide Skye with a little competition, among other things. And as Dallan took Astrid's other daughter, Embla, upon her arm, she thought it was perhaps those "other things" that would do Skye the most good.

Skye walked to the row of bows lining the rack. Many women greeted her as she passed, and she was pleased that names and faces were returning to her. And she was comforted by the fact that those she didn't recognize probably were from out of town.

The bows were all wonderfully crafted, but one in particular caught her eye. It was unique amongst the long and short bows on the rack, for it occupied a space somewhere in between. It was longer than a short bow, but not quite as long as the sturdier weapons. Its curve was graceful, again a balance between the two weapons. And its design was different, with a smooth craftsmanship that was distinctly Tavinter. Skye lifted the weapon from the rack and ran her fingers down the surface.

"This is my bow," she murmured. It was as solid a moment she had experienced since her memories began flooding back at first sight of Dallan. She smiled to herself. "This is my bow."

"That's a beautiful weapon."

Skye glanced up at the loveliness that was Astrid's daughter, the one who was a warrior.

"I'm Eira," she said, extending her hand, and Skye grasped her forearm to forearm in the traditional greeting between Ha'kan warriors.

"I'm Skye," Skye said, then blushed. "But I guess you already knew that."

"Are you going to compete?" Eira said, pointing at the preparations for the archery contest. It was popular for the Ha'kan to fire at small, tarry balls of hay that were launched from miniature catapults as practice. Some targets were already flying through the air, and women were taking turns playfully knocking them down.

"I don't think so," Skye said. "I'm really out of practice."

Skye recognized several members of the Royal Guard who were bringing down the targets with considerable skill. The unique insignia on their armor brought Skye's gaze back to Eira.

"You're a member of the Royal Guard!" Skye exclaimed.

"I am," Eira said with both pride and humility. Skye was used to such contradictions with the Ha'kan, for they were always proud of the collective while minimizing their individual achievements.

"But you're not assigned to the castle."

"No," Eira said, "I have a very special assignment. It's the duty of my unit to protect the former High Priestess, who has retired to her childhood home. It's more of a formality for she's practically worshipped there, and no harm would ever come to her."

"That's wonderful," Skye said.

Eira drew her bow and took a place on the line. She began firing with a methodical skill as she continued talking.

"I hope to eventually protect the Queen and her staff. That would be a great honor."

Skye, too, took the line, but she was nervous. Eira was skilled even for the very talented Royal Guard, and Skye hadn't fired a bow in months. She frowned. She had been sitting around eating chocolates and sipping tea with her mortal enemy. This thought made her even more distracted, and the bow hung limply in her hand.

Senta stood next to one of the nearest catapults and watched her First Ranger stand there indecisively. She was joined by Rika who frowned and crossed her arms over her chest. Even Torsten slipped up beside her, his approach silent until he made himself known.

"That's not good," he muttered. "She's thinking too much."

"Torsten," Senta said thoughtfully, "what say we turn a few of these catapults around?"

Torsten did not at first see what she was getting at, but then he understood. "Better make it five or six. And light the missiles on fire."

Senta raised an eyebrow at Torsten's ruthless raising of the stakes, but he knew Skye better than anyone. She signaled the operators of the two catapults nearest her, who looked at her as if she had lost her mind. Rika and Torsten adjusted two others. The flight paths of the poised missiles were altered, the balls were ignited, then all waited for Senta's signal.

Eira paused on the line, catching sight of the curious actions of the First General. Skye was oblivious, staring at a patch of dirt in front of her with a frown on her face. She was entirely someplace else, that much was certain. Which is why Eira was more than a little concerned when Senta gave a signal and suddenly five balls of fire were flying right at Skye. She tensed to tackle the Tavinter to get her out of the way.

But that was not necessary as the bow came up as if it possessed a will of its own. An arrow was notched and flying while a second appeared to leave the bow almost at the same time. Both arrows flew true, in opposite directions, impaling and redirecting the balls of flame that came from either side. A third arrow was already in the air, this one dead center to where two of the targets converged, impaling both with such force the single arrow reversed their course. It did not appear that Skye would get off the fourth arrow, however, and the ball of flame was near to striking her when she simply took a stance, then thrust the arrow forward as if it were a sword, cleanly impaling the flaming ball of tar and hay and stopping it instantly. She stared at the missile on the end of her arrow as the fire smoked, then went out, and a slow smile spread across her features.

All on the line had stopped in astonishment at a feat none thought they could replicate, one that the Tavinter had accomplished with ease. Skye dropped the arrow to the ground and snuffed out the remaining flame with her boot.

"You were a little slow on that last one," Senta called out across the field, which caused much laughter amongst the Royal Guard and a lot of shaking heads. They knew the formidable First General was as impressed as they were.

"I'll try harder next time, First General," Skye called back.

"Welcome back, First Ranger," one of the Royal Guard called out, a sentiment echoed throughout the field.

Eira moved back next to Skye on the line. "So, that's 'out of practice' for you?"

"Well," Skye said, feeling her confidence returning, "maybe I'm not as rusty as I thought."

The entire day was play. Skye spent some time on the archery range, joyfully challenging Torsten to games they made up, just as they did when they were children. Eira joined in, no matter how ridiculous the rules, and Senta was pleased to see the deadly precision of her First Ranger had returned with a vengeance.

Then Dallan and Rika came along, and the play moved to swordsman-ship. The Princess had picked up on Skye's penchant for creating outlandish challenges. Lifa settled into the stands to watch and Skye waved to her, then blushed profusely, for Lifa was surrounded by Priestesses. Some were from Lifa's own inner circle, Leya, Freya, and Ama, but Astrid flanked Lifa on one side and on the other was a woman as magnetic as the High Priestess. She had her arm around Lifa's waist and Skye recognized Helena, Lifa's mother, from the celebration at the Academy.

The Queen joined the spectators, which only encouraged Dallan to ramp up the exuberant chaos of the free-for-all. Although none equaled Skye with a bow, the sword was Dallan's forte and even Senta was tasked with keeping up with her. Senta had been responsible for much of Dallan's training and was pleased to see her pupil close to surpassing her. Still, the joy of mock battle was not enough to deter the First General from her duties. When she locked swords with Dallan, she leaned in close to whisper to her.

"Do you see the figure over there?"

Dallan nodded, stepped around, and locked swords again. "Yes. I've been watching her for some time. Do you know who she is?"

"No," Senta said with some concern.

The figure was doing nothing out of the ordinary, rather was just leaning against a stone wall with her arms crossed over her chest. There was nothing threatening in her stance. But she was fully hooded so that her features were hidden, unlike everyone else present, and the clothing itself did not lend itself to easy identification. It was plain, neither Tavinter nor Ha'kan, but perhaps elven in origin. Senta could not imagine that anyone could get past the Royal Guard without challenge, and even if they did get past the Royal Guard, they would not evade the Tavinter who detected everything. But until very recently, there had been a contract with the Assassin's Guild to kill a head of state, and the Queen, the Princess, and Skye were all right here. The figure was making Senta uneasy.

"There's one way to find out," Dallan said. She disengaged from Senta and held up her sword, turning about.

"I seek a new a new challenge," she said loudly, "I need a new playmate. How about you?" she said, pointing her sword directly at the cloaked figure. There was a moment of silence at the strange calling out, and Skye stopped her current engagement with Eira and felt a finger of unease trace itself along her spine. Very slowly, the figure pushed away from the wall, and just as slowly lowered the hood.

Dallan dropped her sword into the dust. "I yield."

Senta stabbed her sword into the soft earth, a grin on her features. "As do I."

And the Ha'kan as one breathed out the name, and even the High Priestess herself murmured it with such pleasure it caused Helena to glance over at her in surprise.

"Raine."

Skye's reaction was far less subdued. "Raine!" she cried and rushed the Scinterian warrior. She would have tackled the woman were Raine not solid as stone. Instead, Raine spun her about then set her on her feet, hugging her tightly.

"I'm so glad to see you," Raine said. She brushed Skye's fair hair from her eyes. "And I'm so sorry I couldn't come for you."

"'Tis no matter," Skye said excitedly, "Dallan, Rika, Torsten, Idonea, even Syn, they all came for me."

"As I knew they would," Raine said, clapping Dallan and Rika on the back as they joined the reunion. She clasped arms with the First General as Senta greeted the Scinterian warrior, then was enveloped by a welcoming phalanx of the Royal Guard.

"So that's the Dragon's Lover," Helena said, leaning across her daughter to address the High Priestess without taking her eyes from the newcomer.

"Oh, yes," Astrid said.

"I must say, the legend does not do her justice."

And indeed, it did not, for Raine was the product of a Scinterian father and an Arlanian mother, two extraordinary races that had passed from the world. The Scinterians, allies of the dragons and the most fearsome warriors of all time, and the Arlanians, a gentle people so sexually desirable they were annihilated by the lust of others, these were the races that had produced the impossible melding that was Raine. Helena admired the creature in front of her: lithely muscular, golden hair, dark blue eyes, chiseled features, and understood why she captivated her people.

Raine approached the Queen, who had risen from the stands and stepped down onto the field.

"I beg your forgiveness, your Majesty. I should have presented myself more formally, but they seemed like they were having so much fun."

Halla gave the deep curtsy she would give only to others of equal stature, and although Raine was not a head of state, she had more than earned the honor. Raine returned the deep bow.

"You're always welcome here, Raine," Halla said. "And as promised, your chambers are just as you left them. Will Talan be joining us?"

"Yes," Raine said, "soon. She left for the north to tie up a few loose ends but should be here within a day or so. It's our intent to ride with you to Mount Alfheim. Well," Raine corrected herself, "Talan will probably fly. I'll ride with you."

"That's generous of you and we welcome your company."

The Queen was joined by the High Priestess and another woman wearing the garbs of the Ministry whom Raine did not recognize, at least initially. Raine took Astrid's hand and brushed a kiss across it, which caused a flicker of violet in Raine's eyes. Helena caught her breath at the lovely color. She had heard rumor of the beauty of Arlanian eyes, but until this moment, had never seen it.

"You're going to get me in trouble, High Priestess," Raine said mischievously, knowing her eyes had nearly displayed.

"Would that were true or even possible," Astrid said, a smile playing about her lips. Flirting with the Arlanian was as enjoyable as it was futile. "Raine, this is Helena, our High Priestess for the eastern territories."

This woman was as seductive as Astrid, and Raine brushed another kiss across Helena's hand. She then examined her closely. "And Lifa's mother, if I'm not mistaken."

"You are correct," Helena said with a gentle smile.

This introduction caused Raine's gaze to seek out Lifa, who still sat in the stands and waved to the beloved Scinterian warrior. Raine experienced a strange sensation, one that reminded her of a small band of imperials in the wilds a quarter of a century ago, a Tavinter scout by the name of Isolde, who was filled with magic she did not use, and carried a child none sensed but Raine. Raine's eyes drifted to Lifa's midsection, although her form had yet to change.

"I see that congratulations are in order."

Lifa beamed with pride, and the Queen was astonished at Raine's insight. For a creature who was immune to magic, Raine's sight at times went beyond magic. Raine offered her arm to the Queen in a gallant gesture, and the Queen accepted the escort. A small entourage settled in behind them, which Senta joined. Raine paused at the younger Ha'kan.

"I'll be back later for that challenge," Raine said to Dallan.

"Of course," Dallan said, "but I reserve the right to call on my companions for help," she said, waving to Rika and Skye.

"I wouldn't have it any other way," Raine said. She examined the charming woman next to Skye, one who possessed a familiar sultriness, then turned to the High Priestess. "I see it's family day all around." She winked at Skye. "Have fun," she said laughing over her shoulder as she escorted the Queen from the field.

Eira was overwhelmed by the cheerful stranger, a novelty for all Ha'kan, but particularly for one with the magnetism and allure of the daughter of the High Priestess. Rika clapped her on the shoulder, recognizing the very pleasant discomposure Raine inspired in all of them.

"Don't worry, you get used to that."

"That seems unlikely. She clearly lives up to her Arlanian heritage, but is she really that good a warrior?"

"Better," Dallan said firmly. "It's difficult to describe the impossible, and Raine manages the impossible all the time."

"But she—, she is—," Eira could hardly get the word out, it was so unfamiliar to their culture.

"Monogamous?" Rika interjected, chuckling. "Yes, much to our despair. But when you meet her lover, you'll understand."

"So, you were able to get the Assassin's Guild to rescind the contract?" Senta asked as Raine settled into the circular seating area around the fire pit in the center of the Queen's forums.

"Yes," Raine said, frowning. "I was able to make a deal with the vampyres to cancel the contract. And yes, it was as sordid as you all are imagining."

"Sordid" wasn't exactly what Senta was imagining.

"And what would the vampyres take in exchange for such a request?"

The question came from Gimle, as she came into the forum, having received word of Raine's arrival. The entourage had diminished to the members of Halla's own staff, Senta and Astrid, as well as Helena. And Raine knew that if Helena was staying in the Queen's forum, an honor beyond compare, Helena had the Queen's trust.

Raine's discomfort was evident. "Their leader," she cleared her throat, "manipulated me to acquire several things she wanted. And in the end, I gave her my blood in exchange for the cancellation of the contract."

Helena lifted her hand to her chest in dismay.

"No, no," Raine said, sensing her train of thought, "I can't be turned to vampyrism. Vampyrism is half-disease, half-magic, and I'm immune to magic."

"Immune to magic?" Helena said. "I've never heard of such a thing. What an incredible gift."

"A gift from my parents," Raine agreed.

Raine's discomfort over her contact with the vampyr was evident, but Gimle's scientific curiosity was too great. "I've read in literature that, although the vampyr bite is painful, it can also be pleasurable."

"Um, that's true," Raine said. "It was a very erotic experience."

"I'm surprised that your love allowed such an experience to proceed," the Queen said.

"She was there for the show," Raine said dryly, and the Ha'kan all nodded as if this were perfectly acceptable. "And she threatened to bite the vampyr in two if things went too far." Raine was thoughtful for a moment, then turned to the Queen. "Halla, the Ha'kan are much more long-lived than the sons and daughters of men. Do you remember the Empress Aesa?"

"Yes," Halla said, and Astrid nodded as well. "The Empress was a lovely young woman who disappeared right after the birth of her son, the current Emperor's father."

"It was under suspicious circumstances, if I recall," Astrid said. "They never found her body, but it was presumed she was murdered."

"Yes," Raine said, who looked younger than all present but was centuries older. "I remember."

"Is there a reason why you ask?" the Queen said.

"No, no," Raine said quickly. "Not really. One of the many 'tasks' I was required to complete was to break into a tomb in Hrafn. It had a very powerful seal that none could get past. And in a bit of coincidence, I discovered the seal was placed there by Isleif decades ago."

"It's astonishing how small Arianthem can be at times," Senta commented.

"Agreed. There was a treasure inside, one that the vampyr wanted, and the treasure was from the Farlein dynasty, which made me think of the Empress. The whole thing was incredibly strange," Raine said, contemplating the entire adventure. "At one point in time, the price on my head was larger than all the heads of state's combined."

"And why do I have the feeling that was intentional on your part?" Senta asked, taking a glass of wine offered by an attendant.

"Because you know me, First General," Raine said, also taking a glass. She raised it to Senta. "They can't very well kill anyone else if they're all trying to kill me."

"And Talan was successful with the dragons?" the Queen asked.

Raine took a long drink of the crisp white wine. "More than successful, although it nearly ended in disaster. She easily outwitted the two Ancients who fought against her in the Great War, anticipated their every move. But she didn't foresee the Goddess interfering."

The Scinterian's tan skin paled slightly and Halla knew of whom she spoke.

"Hel was there?"

"Not there," Raine said. "But she gave Volva restraints that Talan couldn't escape, and they nearly drained the life from her. It was why Idonea had to abandon her rescue of Skye, to save her mother. Thank the gods Skye is so skilled."

"And Skye can thank Idonea for that skill, or at least its development," Gimle said, "so she hardly abandoned her."

They were all still piecing together the various events that had occurred across a wide swathe of the continent. "I stopped in to see Y'arren on my way here. She described the spell that Skye cast, hiding thirty people from sight and making them untouchable. Unbelievable."

"Dallan said the wood elves saved them when Skye could no longer maintain the spell," Halla said. "I would like to send Y'arren a gift and hoped you would help me find something suitable."

Raine was thoughtful. "Y'arren wants and needs little. She values material goods and wealth not at all. But she's very fond of tea and sweets, and from what I've sampled, the Ha'kan specialize in both. You needn't send much; it'll be the thought that pleases her."

"Then perhaps we should send a little, but on a regular basis."

Raine smiled, for the Ha'kan were so elegantly perfect about such things. "I think she'd like that."

"So, although we succeeded at everything, there are still some loose threads out there," Senta said.

"Yes," Raine said. "The Alliance is still strong. The dragons are firmly with Talan. But three things bother me. Talan's son, Drakar, killed Jörmung, one of the Ancients who stood against Talan, but Volva, the worst of the two, escaped. And from what Y'arren relayed of Skye's adventure, the sorceress, Ingrid, lives as well."

The women mulled over these unfortunate survivals.

"And the third thing?" Senta asked.

"Those restraints," Raine said, her countenance darkening. "If Hel truly wanted to imprison Talan, she would have used them herself, not given them to Volva and Jörmung."

"Then why did she do so?"

"Because," Raine said with certainty, "she was testing them."

Raine settled into her suite which, as Halla had promised, was exactly as they left it months ago. Although she was as comfortable lying on her knapsack in the middle of the forest as she was in the luxury of a castle, the hospitality of the Ha'kan was unparalleled.

The Queen's forum was laid out in a circle and all the suites opened inside to the center of the common area around the fire pit, and outside onto the Queen's private terrace. Raine pushed through the stained-glass door onto the marbled verandah outside and walked to the stone wall that edged the upper deck. She leaned against the railing, watching the festivities below. Her eyesight was acute, and from her elevated position, she could look all the way across the city. There was some sort of commotion on the main gate leading into Haldis, and Raine shielded her eyes from the sun for a better view.

Senta came up beside her, also shielding her eyes. The Tavinter Rangers were able to pass messages over large distances using signals of reflected light. It was one more thing the Ha'kan had adopted from their new allies, having quickly seen the benefit of the speed of transmission over the common courier. Senta was not as accomplished as the Tavinter, but she was able to interpret this short message.

"A dragon is coming," she said. "I thought you said Talan was not due until tomorrow?"

"Perhaps she finished early," Raine replied. "That's good news."

They were joined by the Queen, Gimle, Astrid, and Helena.

"A dragon is coming," Senta told them.

"Wonderful," Halla exclaimed, "Talan could not stay away from you."

Raine again shielded her eyes, now able to see the form in the clouds, although still very far away. As the massive creature slowly grew larger, a slight look of concern crossed her features.

"I don't think that's Talan," Raine said uncertainly. She could not be sure, for the dragon was still too far away to make out color or shape. But the movement of the wings, something as distinctive for a dragon as gait was for a person, was different.

"Is it Drakar?" Senta asked, trying to gauge the Scinterian's mood. Raine was not overly concerned, just bemused.

"Well it could be anyone," Raine said, "Now that Talan has reconnected with her kind, I'm certain there'll be far more sightings."

"But—?" Senta prompted.

"Drakar is large for his kind," Raine said with a trace of unease, "And that dragon is too big to be Drakar."

"Should we sound the alarm?" Senta asked.

Raine's eyes strained as the creature came closer, seeking any detail that would give her a clue to the dragon's identity. Then, as luck would have it, a ray of sunshine fell on the dragon's hide, and it gave a blue flash, almost like the twinkle of a star.

"No," Raine said with a slow grin, watching the dragon approach, "that won't be necessary. But I should probably warn all of you," she said with a chuckle. "You're in a very different kind of danger."

The dragon was now close enough for all of them to see, and it was a beautiful creature. Iridescent blue scales shimmered in the sunlight, giving off little sparkles of silver light. Raine waved and stepped to the center of the terrace. The dragon circled once, hovered slightly just above Raine, then alighted with considerable grace, although its size was sufficient to shake the thick walls. Then, with a flash of silver light, the dragon disappeared and was replaced by an exquisite woman in a blue gown the same color and pattern as her scales. It was a gorgeous ensemble, befitting the woman who wore it, whose ice blue eyes were framed so perfectly by long dark hair streaked with silver.

"Hello, my little Scinterian."

To the astonishment of the Ha'kan, the woman pulled Raine to her, kissed her in a manner that was hardly chaste, then released her. To their even greater astonishment, Raine's eyes were pure violet, a response that none but Talan engendered, and the warrior blushed profusely.

"I see that Raine likes her dragons," Helena murmured to Astrid. Prior to that moment, it had seemed the Scinterian was as immune to the attentions of others as she was to magic.

"Yes, she does," Astrid murmured back, as surprised as her Priestess.

"You're going to get me in trouble," Raine said for the second time in a day. She willed her eyes back to the light blue color of her father's people.

"Untrue, unfortunately," Kylan said. "And quite impossible. You're faithful beyond belief. And Talan is the only one in this world who possesses the whole of my loyalty."

Raine took her by the hand. "And I can't express enough gratitude for that loyalty. Talan told me how you stood by her side."

"Hmm," Kylan said, "gratitude. That is in fact why I'm here."

"How so?" Raine asked as Kylan's eyes flicked past her to the women standing on the terrace.

"I was going to return to my castle, but it was Talan who suggested I might come down and acquaint myself with the natives. A bit of a vacation as a reward, if you will."

"You've never been to the land of the Ha'kan?" Raine asked.

"Not for centuries. Like most of our kind, I spent a very long time sleeping after the Great War."

"Then you're in for a treat," Raine said. "And I'm sure they'll welcome you with open arms."

Open arms, and slightly open mouths, greeted the Ancient Dragon as Raine escorted her to the Royal Staff. They regained their composure, however, and Queen Halla stepped forward to offer a gracious greeting.

"Your Majesty," Raine said, "This is Kylan'ilaith'alnon, Talan's ally and Second."

The Queen bowed. "The Ha'kan are honored to claim Talan as ally and friend. Our home is open to you."

"Thank you, your Majesty," Kylan said, examining each of the women at length. "I think my stay here will be most pleasant."

Halla gestured to the doorway that led to the common area of her forum. "You're welcome to stay in one of the guest rooms of my forum. There's one right next to Talan's quarters, and my staff will be at your service."

Raine grinned at the sexually charged conversation taking place between the Queen of the Ha'kan and the Ancient Dragon. Senta hung back.

"So, is Kylan...?"

"Available?" Raine proffered, easily reading the First General's mind. "Oh yes. Kylan belongs only to herself. Although I warn you, the lust of dragons is not a myth, and it might take the lot of you to keep her satisfied."

This statement was impossible to fathom.

"Your Majesty," Kylan said, her voice drifting back to them, "have you ever ridden a dragon?"

Senta appeared to be choking on something.

"Go," Raine said, laughing at the First General's attempted restraint. "Go before you have a heart attack."

Raine returned to her chambers but was too restless to stay. Seeing Kylan made her long for Weynild, and she hoped that her love would arrive soon.

She decided to take Dallan up on her challenge and went to find the younger Ha'kan. Dallan, Skye, and Rika had been joined by Astrid's daughter, the one who was a warrior, and two others. The slender one with the light hair bore a remarkable resemblance to the First Scholar, and Raine surmised this was Gimle's daughter. The other wore training gear associated with the Scholar caste, which was not unusual to see on the Ha'kan training grounds for all castes were welcome. What was unusual was the size of this scholar and the skill with which she wielded a sword and shield. Or perhaps not, Raine mused, when she noted that the scholar looked a great deal like the First General.

Lifa greeted Raine warmly as the Scinterian settled onto the bench next to her.

"You're not going to go play with them?" she asked.

"Of course, I am," Raine said, "I thought I might visit with you a moment."

"Raine, this is Embla," Lifa said, leaning back and gesturing to the woman on her right.

"Ah," Raine said, "one of Astrid's daughters." The woman was several years older than Lifa and was already displaying signs of her mother's poise and sultry elegance. Raine took the hand she extended, and Embla stifled a gasp at the touch. She marveled at the sensation the simple contact produced. Although she lived in a world imbued with sensuality, she had never experienced anything quite like the touch of an Arlanian. It inspired instant sexual desire, almost a craving, and Embla understood more the legend of the beautiful but doomed people.

"I'm sorry," Raine said, "I forget when I meet new people that my touch can be unsettling."

Embla smiled. "It's unsettling in a most pleasant manner. There's no need to apologize."

"It's rare for a Priestess to be caught off-guard in such a way," Lifa said, agreeing, "and it is pleasing."

Raine's eyes dropped to Lifa's stomach, and her expression grew very gentle. "Might I?"

Lifa moved the hand that was resting there. "Of course."

Raine settled her hand on Lifa's stomach and a beatific smile settled on her chiseled features. For Lifa, the touch was extraordinary and so many pleasant sensations shot through her that she didn't want Raine to move her hand, ever. And amazingly, the tiny being inside her gave a kick for the very first time, and she felt the movement.

"Did you feel that?" Lifa said, excited.

"I did!" Raine exclaimed. "How wonderful!"

Raine removed her hand and Lifa felt the loss keenly, but only for a second until Embla leaned forward and placed her own hand on Lifa's stomach. The Priestess might not have been Arlanian, but she possessed all of her mother's allure, and the touch was just as welcome. Perhaps even more welcome, for Raine could not satisfy the longing her touch elicited, whereas Embla certainly could. She brushed Lifa's hair from her eyes.

"Perhaps you should go rest," she suggested, "I'll walk you to your chambers."

Raine grinned. "I think that's an excellent idea. I'll go play with Dallan."

Eyes turned to the Scinterian when she strolled out onto the field. Rika glanced past her to the departing Priestesses, and she, too, grinned. She was pretty sure Lifa wasn't going to get much rest with that gorgeous daughter of Astrid. Both Embla and Eira were just enough older than them to inspire huge crushes when they were younger, infatuations that had not waned with adulthood.

"Who was that dragon?" Dallan asked. "We saw it come in and land on the terrace."

"That was Kylan. She is one of the remaining Ancients and Talan's Second, absolutely loyal to my love."

"Another Ancient?" Skye asked, her eyes glowing at the thought.

Rika nudged Dallan in the ribs. "Someone else for you to stumble about."

Dallan frowned, for that most certainly was true. She had effortlessly charmed women her entire life, but completely fell apart around Talan, almost always blushing and barely able to get a word out. Her seductive daughter, although not a dragon, had the same effect on her. It was mortifying.

Eira and Solvi were both intrigued by this. Dallan had flirted with them shamelessly even as a child and had become a polished and talented courtesan as an adult. It would be humorous to see her in such a predicament because it was so at odds with her natural state.

"So...," Rika began, and Raine knew where she was going.

"Kylan is tied to no one, and I'm sure she'll fully partake in Ha'kan hospitality."

"Really?" Dallan said, her voice cracking in the middle of the word, causing Skye to muffle a snort of laughter and Rika to laugh out loud.

"Really," Raine said. "Although I think you're going to have to wait in line because she left on your mother's arm with the entire Royal Staff in tow."

"So, the sexual prowess of dragons is not exaggerated?"

This question came from the scholar, the one that resembled the First General.

"I beg your pardon," Dallan said, remembering her manners. "Raine, this is Runa, Senta's daughter. Solvi is Gimle's daughter, and Eira is Astrid's."

Raine grasped forearms with each of them. "I could have guessed. You all look very much like your mothers. And no, the lust and skill of the dragons is not exaggerated."

"That's fascinating," Runa said, staring at her forearm. She had already moved on from her question because the sensation the touch produced was extraordinary.

"I would say that you get you used to it," Dallan said, "but you don't."

"Are we going to train?" Raine said, playfully shoving the Princess.

And so, the mêlée began. The Scinterian drew double swords and easily fended off Dallan's attack. Rika came in from the side, but the swords were there to block her. Skye came in with two daggers, but Raine's short swords were just as fast and the Tavinter speed was of no use against the flurry. Eira sought to move in for a blow but Raine was very good at lining up her opponents so that they all got in one another's way. Attempts to surround her were futile because she was always moving. The Royal Guard were enjoying the show and cheering everyone on. Solvi stepped in her way, thinking to trap Raine against a hay cart, but Raine nimbly danced up the side of the cart, balancing on the sides as she parried Runa's strikes, the only one tall enough to reach Raine at that height. The Ha'kan were all laughing as the Scinterian was able to make them stumble against one another. Such a display might have been humiliating from any other opponent, but this was a warrior who fought as one of the gods. And Raine's good-natured play drew only merriment from her challengers. With a great leap, she cleared the mass and stood with her swords raised, on the ground once more.

Then an enormous shadow passed over her head, her blue and gold markings rose to the surface on her skin, and she raised her swords to a far more dangerous opponent.

"Well this is hardly fair," she muttered.

The dragon swooped around in a great arc, spraying fire in a circle around Raine and isolating her from all others. Eira felt a stab of fear and looked to Dallan for some sort of cue as to how to respond. But Dallan, Skye, and Rika merely stood with their swords dangling from their hands, looks of awe on their faces. The dragon came around again in a tight arc and looked as if it might land right on top of the Scinterian, but at the last moment, a brilliant flash of yellow light blinded them all. When Eira's sight returned, a magical scene greeted her.

In the center of the fiery circle, the Scinterian was pinned to the ground by an extraordinary woman in fiery red armor. Her hair was silver, and her eyes were amber. She was stunning, elegant, and regal, and she held the Scinterian effortlessly when half a Ha'kan regiment had been unable to touch her. The woman looked down on her captive with amusement while Raine looked at her with equal parts embarrassment and adoration: embarrassed because she was so easily captured, and adoration because only her love was capable of such an act. The silver-haired woman kissed her deeply and Raine ardently returned the kiss. When her eyes re-opened, they were pure violet, a purple that would put the finest lavender to shame.

"That seemed a practiced maneuver," Rika murmured.

Talan stood upright in a lithe movement that belied her apparent age. "Apparent," because all dragons were skilled shapeshifters and she could manifest in any form she chose. But she chose to manifest in a form consistent with her lifespan, which already exceeded a millennium. Raine had fallen in love with both forms upon first sight. Talan helped her to her feet, pulling the warrior upright as if she weighed nothing.

"That maneuver did require a great deal of practice," Talan said over her shoulder, and Rika swallowed hard. She had forgotten how acute the dragon's hearing was. "The first time nearly ended in disaster."

Raine grinned. "Yes, if I remember rightly, you transformed a bit late and nearly crushed me to death."

Talan leaned down and kissed her again. "It's fortunate you're so indestructible."

The fire was dying down and the two stepped over the now-smoking grass. Skye was closest to the pair and she bowed deeply, a sign not of just respect, but one of near worship.

"And how are you, little Tavinter?"

"I'm fine, your Majesty. Idonea came to save me."

Talan examinèd the young woman. "From what I understand, you saved yourself, as well as many others."

"But I couldn't have done it without Idonea's teaching."

"Teaching which must continue. My daughter is on her way here now."

The dimples appeared in Skye's cheeks. "I can't wait to see her!"

Talan's amber eyes flicked to Rika, who bowed deeply, then to Eira, Runa, and Solvi. The latter three were frozen under the penetrating gaze of the dragon. Talan's gaze at last settled on Dallan, who turned bright red under the scrutiny.

"Your Highness," Talan said.

"Your Majesty," Dallan said, bowing deeply while her voice cracked in the middle of the salutation. Skye covered her mouth to muffle laughter. Raine felt sorry for the Princess and sought to rescue her.

"Kylan arrived a few hours ago."

Talan turned her attention back to Raine. And to Dallan's great relief, the rest of the world disappeared when the two were together.

"I should greet her."

"Well, last I saw she was leading an entourage into the Ha'kan baths."

"How predictable," Talan said drily.

"Perhaps we should go greet her together," Raine said mischievously.

The amber eyes glowed. "I'm certain that Kylan 'greeted' you at first opportunity. And if I remember correctly, you were quite disruptive on your last trip to the baths. I think you should run a bath in our room and I'll join you shortly."

Raine offered her hand in escort in a gallant gesture. "I like that idea very much," she said as the two left arm-in-arm.

Eira watched the stunning pair leave. Raine was enthralling all on her own, but the two together were mesmerizing. And that dragon was very possessive of her young lover, that much was clear. She turned to Rika.

"I understand what you said earlier about the two of them. It's foreign to us, but those two are a perfect match."

The Ha'kan baths were a wonder of Arianthem that few had ever seen. Almost everyone had heard of them, rumors abounded, and tales ranged from a sensual paradise to a carnal orgy of flesh. Both portrayals, in a way, were apt, although the descriptions chosen revealed more about the person telling the tale than they did about the Ha'kan.

The baths were like everything else in Ha'kan culture: open, sexual, sensuous, and communal. And because the baths were warm, wet, and steamy, and clothing was optional, they were perhaps even a little more so. There were various private alcoves for trysts, a very public massage area, small bathing pools for couples or threesomes, and then larger pools for groups where women could engage in simple small talk or wrap themselves about one another. One bathing area in particular was attracting considerable attention, for Kylan was holding court with the Queen and her entire staff. The dragon was wickedly funny, unrepentant, and completely uninhibited, and the Ha'kan loved her.

Attention was redirected, however, when a tall, silver-haired woman in red armor strolled through the bathing area. Her heavy, spiked armor was in stark contrast to the soft nudity around her, but that was not what attracted so much attention. This woman strode through the room with a confidence that was magnetic, her amber eyes went where they pleased, and all blushed at the honor of the attention. Powerful sexuality swirled about her much like the dark magic that permeated her being. She stopped at the edge of the pool, gazing down at Kylan.

"Why am I not surprised?"

"Because you know me, my love," Kylan said, her blue eyes twinkling with mirth. She stood, completely naked, water dripping, and stepped up the marble ledge. Although faithful to Raine, that did not stop Talan from a sweeping, appreciative, examination of Kylan's nude form.

"My Queen," Kylan said, embracing her and giving her the same, less-than-chaste kiss she had given Raine, although Raine had not received the added perk of Kylan's bare breasts pressed against her. All Ha'kan watched with pleasure, for it was as pleasing for them to observe the act as it was to participate in it, and any time two women were standing next to one another, the Ha'kan were imagining them in bed. Right now, that picture was very pleasant.

"Are you sure you won't join us?" Kylan teased, knowing the answer.

Talan's gaze swept the bevy of beauties in the bath. "Tempting," Talan said. "But I have a naked Arlanian in my bed, one with the stamina of the ancient dragon slayers. I imagine I'll be busy for the next few hours."

"Understood," Kylan said, laughing, and settled into the bath once more.

"Welcome back to Haldis, Talan," the Queen said as Kylan put her arm around her.

"Thank you, your Majesty," Talan said over her shoulder as she turned to leave. And all Ha'kan contemplated another pleasant picture in their heads, that of the dragon dominating her lover in the chambers above them.

"Kylan is quite at home in the land of the Ha'kan."

Raine was leaning back in the marble bath, one that was the size of a small pool. She silently thanked the dwarves for their past dealings with the Ha'kan, dealings in which they returned an ancient favor by providing their unsurpassed technology. The water was heated via various steam contraptions buried deep in the earth, then piped into the castle.

"I can only imagine the chaos she's creating," Raine said.

"The Ha'kan are enjoying it as much as she is."

A response died on Raine's lips as Weynild's armor retracted and her long limbs, proud breasts, and flat stomach were revealed. In the presence of others, Raine addressed Weynild only by her formal name, but when they were alone together, she used the name she had known her by first.

"What did you say?" Raine asked, completely distracted.

Weynild waded into the water. "It's unimportant."

Raine rose from the water to embrace her and Weynild kissed her passionately. The long limbs guided the Arlanian to the gentle slope where one could lie quite comfortably, and the dragon settled her hips between her young lover's legs while the warm water lapped against them. It was a glorious sensation for Raine: the strength of the woman above her, those magnificent breasts pressed against her wet skin, the taste of those red lips. And it was no less glorious for Weynild, who hungered for her Arlanian as she had no other. It was almost impossible to sate a dragon, yet this little creature managed it without fail. At times, they would engage in foreplay for hours, but today would not be one of those times. There were distinct advantages to being a shapeshifter, especially when it came to lovemaking, and Raine gasped as Weynild utilized this ability and Raine received the benefit as she was penetrated by whatever had struck Weynild's fancy. She nearly swooned at the shock of pleasure. Sometimes their lovemaking was gentle and playful, but today it was a storm of intensity. Weynild's golden eyes bore into hers so she could know exactly the affect her firm thrusts were having. And Raine could not look away, their bond so complete that all else ceased to exist as long as their bodies were locked together. Raine desperately wanted to release, for the smooth, long strokes were driving her to madness, but she could tell that her love was close to losing control as Weynild's rhythm quickened, as did her breathing. Finally, Raine could bear it no longer and allowed the climax to carry her away, and it took only her uninhibited release to drive the dragon to climax as well.

The silver-haired woman collapsed on the muscular form beneath her, and Raine enjoyed the weight and closeness of her lover. She could feel the powerful heartbeat slow, could feel the rise and fall of the chest return to normal. Weynild pulled back, examined the beautiful violet eyes beneath her, then kissed her gently on the lips. Raine returned the gentle kiss, then playfully parted the lips with her tongue.

"You know what you're doing," Weynild said with warning.

"Of course, I do," Raine murmured, deepening the kiss.

"Then you'll have to suffer the consequences."

This threat elicited only laughter from the Scinterian as the dragon gently but firmly turned her over, face down, then began anew.

Skye lie in her bed intertwined with Eira. She had always liked older women, and Eira's seduction of her had been masterful. The beautiful warrior possessed all her mother's magnetism, and although Skye had not slept with the High Priestess, Skye imagined that Eira possessed a great deal of her mother's skill as well.

"Thank you," Skye said shyly, and Eira found the shyness endearing, for it was rare in the Ha'kan.

"There's no need to thank me," Eira said, "I took great pleasure in that." She hugged the slender Tavinter and shifted so that Skye could lie on her chest. A comfortable silence settled upon them.

"Can I ask you a question?"

"Of course," Eira said.

"It's about your sister, Embla. She seems very happy and content. She's not disappointed that she's not the future High Priestess?"

"What?" Eira asked, as if the question made no sense.

"Well, usually, among my people, children follow in their parents' footsteps."

"Oh," Eira said, understanding. "That's the exception for the Ha'kan. Each of us finds our own path, and all are guided from a young age to find the role that will suit them best. And when I say 'best,' I mean the role that will provide us the most happiness and meaning."

"That sounds so wonderful," Skye said. She had spent much time contemplating the unusual society of the Ha'kan, and once again, she wondered how much their unique reproduction and singular sex contributed to the harmony of their culture. Competition was almost always playful, personal ambition nearly non-existent. Relieved of the basic drive of procreation, the Ha'kan existed in a chronic state of contentment. Any threats to their people came from the outside, and Skye was filled with gratitude that the insular people had so accepted her and the Tavinter as a whole.

"Besides," Eira mused, "Embla disappeared with the future High Priestess several hours ago and they've not been seen since. She loves Lifa, and really, who could not?"

Skye grinned at the thought of the two Priestesses together.

"Rika headed off with Solvi," Eira said, "and they'll probably wrestle to see who gets to be earth and sky."

"Solvi's not very big," Skye said doubtfully, "do you think she has a chance against Rika?"

"Solvi is very wily. I wouldn't be surprised if she has Rika on the bottom right now."

Skye giggled at the thought as Eira continued her run-down of the night's pairings. "And Dallan was accosted by both Runa and Kara, so she is in for a night to remember."

"Runa can't be as wild as Kara is," Skye said. Kara was known for her love of the unconventional and her desire to experiment on her sexual partners.

"I'm not certain anyone is as adventurous as Kara," Eira said, "but all scholars have that terrifying bent towards research in the bed."

"That's for certain," Skye agreed, thinking of her trysts with both Kara and Gimle.

"Oh, that's right!" Eira exclaimed. "You've been with the First Scholar. You must tell me all about it!"

And so, in a conversation that most would have found bizarre, but for the Ha'kan was completely normal, the two women described in detail their sexual exploits with others, enjoying the tales almost as much as if they had experienced them firsthand. And ultimately, their discussion led to such arousal they stopped talking about the act and began participating in it.

But perhaps the most content Ha'kan in all the castle were in the Queen's room, where the Ancient Dragon Kylan lay blissfully entangled with a heap of exhausted women. Her Royal Majesty was asleep in one arm while the High Priestess was asleep in the other. The First General had an arm wrapped about Kylan's thigh and the First Scholar had one wrapped about her waist. The High Priestess of the Eastern Region was curled about her hip, sandwiched between the First General and the Queen. And although Kylan was partial to her kind, simply for reasons of stamina, she had to admit that the Ha'kan were in a splendid category all their own.

CHAPTER 3

It was two very contented groups of Ha'kan that breakfasted on the terrace in the morning. The younger Ha'kan started to seat themselves on Dallan's terrace, a mirror-image of the Queen's, but Halla waved her daughter over and the families gathered as one. Additional place settings were brought out, and the Royal Staff and the future Royal Staff dined together. Raine came out, waved, but did not immediately join them, rather walked to the edge of the terrace. She was followed by both Talan and Kylan. The Ha'kan watched curiously as discussion ensued, Raine nodded, and Talan kissed her. Kylan then playfully blew her a kiss, and the two older women moved some distance apart. They simultaneously disappeared into flashes of light, one white, one yellow, and two enormous dragons stood in their place. It was the first time that any present had seen them together, and it was a magnificent sight, the blue dragon with scales that twinkled like starlight and the red dragon that flickered iridescently as if on fire. It was a good thing the Ha'kan palace was a sturdy structure, for both creatures were enormous. Great muscles flexed, tendons tightened, and both dragons leaped into the air, their wings unfurling and catching the light breeze. The red dragon went east, and the blue dragon went west, and it was not long before both disappeared from sight. Raine leaned against the bannister and watched their flight.

"I never realized there was so much excitement in the capital," Helena commented.

Halla dabbed at her mouth. "It was not always so," she said. "But ever since Talan responded to my request for help, the excitement has not stopped."

"It was even before that," Dallan said, "when we were attacked by the Hyr'rok'kin while still at the Academy and Raine came to save us."

"That's right," Halla agreed. "It hasn't really slowed down since then. There have been stretches where things have been mundane, but those are the exception rather than the rule."

"I must say I like it," Helena said.

Senta watched Raine curiously. She assumed Raine would join them once the dragons had departed, but something in the courtyard had caught her attention. She was staring down expectantly, as if waiting for someone. That speculation was proven correct as a raven-haired woman appeared at the top of the circular stairway, embraced Raine, then kissed her on the cheek. The affection between the two women was evident, and the dark-haired mage did not release Raine.

"Speaking of excitement," Senta said, drawing the attention of the others to the reunion.

"Oh, how marvelous," Halla exclaimed, and Helena noted as much delight in the Queen's voice as with the dragons. Helena examined this new-comer, clothed in lovely robes embroidered with arcane symbols. Beneath the robe was a laced bodice that plunged to her navel, a bodice that somehow magically contained the full breasts that threatened to fall out upon her playful mauling of the Scinterian.

"It's a good thing that Talan left," Helena said.

This elicited a chuckle from many at the table. "Talan fully expects that type of behavior from Idonea."

"Ah," Helena said as the identity of the mystery woman became clear. "That's the dragon's daughter."

"You just missed your mother," Raine said, out-of-earshot of the Ha'kan but on the same topic. "She and Kylan left to survey the surrounding countryside."

"That's a good idea. I came across several bands of Hyr'rok'kin on my way here from imperial lands."

Raine gave her a quick once-over. "You look none the worse for wear."

"They were not so lucky," Idonea said.

"Good for you," Raine said with approval. "I might go out scouting later myself. I've been itching for a fight."

"Not me," Idonea said, smoothing her robes. "I want to get cleaned up, rested, then get back to work with my little protégé."

"She'll be thrilled," Raine said, offering her arm to Idonea.

The Ha'kan had remained respectfully at a distance, but all rose as the two approached. The Queen held out her hands and Idonea took them in her own.

"Idonea, welcome back. Your chambers in Dallan's forum are untouched if you wish to stay there."

Idonea sent a smoldering glance Dallan's way, who true to form, blushed bright red, causing her usual companions to snicker and her recent companions to shake their heads in astonishment.

"That would be wonderful, your Majesty. I'll get settled, and then you and I," she said, turning to Skye, "have to get back to work."

"I can't wait!" Skye exclaimed.

Idonea turned to the First Scholar. "Would you care to join us for lessons?"

A cool smile crossed Gimle's delicate features. "I would be delighted."

"Excellent," Idonea said, "this afternoon, then."

"Come along, Baroness," Raine said, "I'll escort you to your suite."

Idonea's laughter drifted backward as the two left the terrace. The salutation was a great joke between the two of them, Idonea having acquired it when Raine gave her Fireside, the most luxurious residence in the imperial capital.

"Let me tell you the fun I had with that title..."

After a brief respite, Idonea found Raine and the two walked together to the Scholar's wing of the castle.

"So how goes your little fling with the Knight Commander?"

"It continues as it started, wild and unexpected. She appears to have accepted my inability to commit to a single person." Raine looked unconvinced, so Idonea continued. "Oh, Nerthus is certainly jealous, but if she doesn't hear of it or see it, she doesn't ask."

"Ah," Raine said. She changed the subject, growing serious. "Do you think you could have defeated Ingrid?"

Twenty years ago, Idonea's response would have been arrogant, bragging, and likely untrue. Much had changed in the two decades she had spent as Isleif's protégé.

"I believe so," she said in a measured response. "That sorceress is powerful and very skilled, but I think I could have outlasted her. My mother's blood is a deep well of magic."

Raine nodded her understanding. Idonea was the product of Talan's mating with a human male, and therefore not a dragon. Dragons could only be produced by mating with another dragon, as was Talan's son Drakar. But Idonea benefitted from the dark magic that flowed through the dragons, and the fact that she had trained with one of the greatest wizards Arianthem had ever known had magnified and focused that power. Once redirected from her selfish pursuits and adolescent angst, Idonea had become a splendidly talented mage.

Idonea stopped and Raine stopped with her.

"There is something I wanted to talk to you about."

"And what's that?"

"Those restraints that were on my mother."

Raine's expression grew grim. "Ah, yes. The gift from the Goddess."

Idonea leaned close and grasped Raine's arm, emphasizing the weight of her concern. "First off, they were mere filaments, strands, little more than a bracelet. If they had been any larger, I'm not sure I could have broken them."

Raine sighed heavily. "And it's certain Hel is working on something larger."

"More importantly," Idonea said, "there was some dark magic in them, but very little. They were made of something else, and their power is not magical in origin."

"So, it's not likely I could disenchant them," Raine said. She leaned on the marble railing of the walkway, staring at nothing. "The gods have a power all their own. Hel can immobilize me, but it's as if she saps my will. It's not magic."

"Perhaps it's something similar, then," Idonea said.

"Perhaps." A muscle worked in Raine's jaw as she wrestled with demons that Idonea could only imagine.

Raine sighed again and pushed away from the railing. "Then we just have to make sure the restraints stay off your mother."

The two started walking, attracting many admiring looks from the Royal Guard they passed. The fair-haired Scinterian and the dark-haired mage were a study in gorgeous contrast. Raine was unaware of the scrutiny, still mulling over the restraints, but Idonea cast many flirtatious glances along their path. It was not long before they reached the Scholar's wing.

Gimle was waiting for them in her annex, and they no sooner arrived than Skye rushed in with Kara and Runa.

"I hope you don't mind my presence," Runa said, bowing to the First Scholar. "I have no magical skill of my own, but there's a young woman in my cohort, fresh from the Academy, who has shown some promise. I'd like to help her."

"That's wonderful," Gimle said warmly. The Ha'kan were not naturally skilled at magic and most had no ability whatsoever. Gimle was a rare exception and acted not only as the First Scholar, but as the Queen's battle mage. Kara, her successor, had no penchant for magic, so Skye's unexpected ability was considered a gift from the gods, for it was assumed she would act as Dallan's battle mage. "You're most welcome."

All settled into the cushioned, circular seating area.

"Now Skye," Idonea began. "I want you to tell me about the invisibility spell, and more importantly, about its second half."

"Okay," Skye said, thinking back to the events with the sorceress. "Right after you had to leave, Ingrid turned on us. I knew we didn't have a chance, so I pulled everyone close and made us invisible."

"An illusion spell?" Runa asked with interest.

"No," Gimle answered. "I've seen Skye do this before and I'm highly resistant to illusion magic. It's not done by influencing the mind. It's pure light magic."

"We couldn't be seen," Skye explained, "but we could be heard, and we could be hurt. Here, watch."

And without hesitation, Skye cast the spell upon herself and disappeared. Runa stared in astonishment, then jumped when Skye's voice came from where she was still seated.

"I'm still here, you can touch me."

Tentatively, Runa reached out and felt the area where Skye had been. Her hand brushed what felt like an arm, and she grasped it in wonder.

Skye reappeared. "So that's the first half of the invisibility spell."

"You used to use visualization to cast spells," Idonea said. "It didn't look like you needed it just then."

Skye was thoughtful. "No, you're right. I used to imagine hiding in the forest, but now I just feel a surge of emotion."

Idonea nodded her understanding. "Good, that's a major advancement. Now what happened next with the sorceress?"

"We put some distance between her and us, because she began flinging fire and ice around. Then she opened a portal and Reaper Shards came through when she left."

All paled at the mention of the monstrosities, all except Raine and Idonea, who merely grew grim because they had killed more than their fair share of the foul creatures.

"We were trapped, and they could sense us. They came right for us. When they were almost upon us, Dallan remembered that Isleif had given her a message, the word 'ephemeral.'"

Idonea leaned forward. "And then what happened?"

Skye's gaze was distant, her eyes on a battlefield of a ruined garden. "When she spoke the word, I heard Isleif's voice, and I knew instantly what to do. The words just came to me in my head, in a language I don't even think I know."

"Can you remember the words?" Raine asked.

The words came out slowly, primeval and arcane. Gimle cocked her head to one side. She was fluent in multiple languages, but this one was not familiar. "It sounds Elvish, but I don't recognize any of the words."

Idonea looked to the only one who would, and Raine nodded.

"It's the Ancient tongue, an elven language forgotten even by the elves themselves."

"But you speak it," Runa said in admiration.

"I am goddaughter to Y'arren," Raine explained, "the matriarch of the wood elves. She taught me years ago." Raine turned the attention back to Skye. "So, you were able to grasp this spell from one word and repeat it in a nearly dead language you don't even know."

Skye furrowed her brow. "It sounds very hard when you put it that way. It was more like I just understood. The Reaper Shards were almost on us, I drew everyone close and made us ephemeral."

"What's the difference between invisible and ephemeral?" Kara asked.

"Let me show you," Skye said, and again effortlessly cast an impossible spell.

The Tavinter disappeared, and Kara reached forward to touch her. But this time, her hand simply passed through the space where Skye had been. When she sat back, Skye reappeared exactly where Kara's hand had just been.

"You need to be a little careful with that," Raine cautioned, "if you had reappeared when Kara's hand was still there, that could have been a problem."

"I thought about that when we were running through the forest," Skye said. "We were running right through trees, and if I had lost control of the spell, that could have been a disaster."

"And you were able to add the rest of your band, almost thirty people total, to your ephemeral spell, while you were running through the forest?" Idonea asked.

"I got tired very quickly," Skye confessed, "and Rika had to carry me."

Raine suppressed a grin. Skye was confessing to a nonexistent weakness, for it was likely she was the only one who could cast such a spell, let alone do so while fleeing from a horde of Hyr'rok'kin.

"Did you have to touch the other members of your band to add them to the spell?"

This had not occurred to Skye before. "No," she said in surprise, "I didn't. We were running right for them and there was no time."

"Excellent," Idonea said, pleased. "That's another major advancement. All your crutches are being removed and you're moving toward an expression of pure magic."

Skye contemplated this milestone. "So, I don't need to physically connect with someone to include them in my spell."

"Apparently not," Idonea said. "Cast the invisibility spell on everyone here."

Skye did so, and everyone but Raine disappeared.

"And of course, nothing works on our Scinterian," Idonea's voice said. "Skye, now cast the ephemeral spell."

To Raine's vantage point, nothing changed. But no one was speaking and the room was silent and still. Out of curiosity, she reached to her right and left and made both Idonea and Gimle reappear. And when she reached out and touched Skye, everyone reappeared.

"That's amazing," Skye said, speaking of Raine's ability and not her own.

"It's extraordinary, isn't it?" Idonea said, knowing exactly what Skye was talking about. She had more than once experienced it herself. "So much magic and power, then suddenly, it's just gone."

Raine chuckled. "Believe it or not, I once took that ability for granted. When I was young and training with the last of the Scinterians, it seemed little more than a novelty. It wouldn't stop a sword or an arrow, or even a punch to the face. It felt almost useless. But after three centuries, I can say it's the greatest gift I have."

Raine left Skye to Idonea's tutelage and thought to roam about the nearby countryside. It was unlikely that Talan or Kylan had left any Hyr'rok'kin for her, but she could find some game if nothing else. Although she could have found numerous companions to accompany her, Raine decided a little solitude would do her good. She quietly informed the guards at the south gate of her intention, then slipped away soundlessly into the forest.

After trudging for some time without finding any game, Raine admitted to herself she wasn't really looking. Her bow was still folded at her belt, the arrows still quivered, and the swords still sheathed. She walked noiselessly, but not with the stealth required to hunt. A rustle of leaves in the brush next to her caught her attention, and she spoke to the interloper.

"Come on out."

A young wolf crawled from the underbrush, got to his feet, and shook the leaves from his coat. He trotted over to her, then fell into stride next to her. Raine welcomed his company.

"I thought I was going to hunt," Raine said, "but I guess I'm not in the mood."

The wolf was content just to lope at her side, and Raine again fell into silence. Her mood at the moment was contemplative, even a little gloomy, something that would have been evident to those around her, and she did not want her temperament to influence them. It was crucial that she appear as confident and cheerful as always.

But although she felt confident, Raine was hardly cheerful. She felt an oppression, a great pressure, a darkness looming on the horizon like a deadly storm. It was the hand of fate that was coming down to crush her, or worse, pluck her up and carry her away.

Raine shook her head to clear it. "I need to stop thinking like that."

The wolf glanced up at her quizzically but continued to lope along. He stopped when Raine stopped, and although he did not sense what she sensed, he sat down on his haunches patiently.

"What is this?" she murmured.

It felt familiar, something she had met once before. She cocked her head to one side and now she could hear it. The low rumbling breath of something very large. The wolf, too, could hear it, and the hair on the back of his neck raised ever-so-slightly. He was not fearful, just wary, and he stood up and stepped forward when Raine did.

Raine pushed through the trees toward the low rumbling, and it grew louder as she neared. She could see the creature through the tangle of branches, the opal-white scales that glowed. She stepped into the clearing, and the deep blue eyes of the white dragon assessed her at length. They slid to her wolf companion.

"Fenrir's children adore you," the dragon said, "but he cannot help you."

"I know that," Raine said calmly. "Can you?"

The dragon was expressionless, and her tone was impartial. "I cannot."

"Then why are you here?" Raine demanded.

"To convince you to run. You and your dragon lover could find a place to hide."

"Run away? And abandon the people of Arianthem to the Hyr'rok'kin?"

"They will abandon you."

The words were chillingly matter of fact.

"I don't believe that," Raine said, "and even if it's true, I don't care. I won't let the weakness of others dictate my path. I will make my own destiny."

The dragon's nostrils flared slightly as she took a deep breath. "Do you even know your destiny, the fourth line of the prophecy?"

"No," Raine said angrily, "and I don't care. It won't make any difference."

"And that's where you're wrong, Scinterian." For the first time, the dragon displayed emotion, and it was sadness mixed with regret. "I can assure you that Hel knows the final line."

Raine stood silently, seething at the dragon's words. "And why would Hel be interested in a prophecy supposedly about me? One in which all worlds are saved?"

The blue eyes gazed at her intently. "Because that prophecy was given to Hel. Eons ago, before you were ever born."

This silenced Raine, for she had no response to words spoken with such authority. There was no question of their truth.

"Who are you?" Raine said at last.

"It doesn't matter," the white dragon said. And with those final words, the creature disappeared.

Raine was leaning against the railing waiting for Talan when she returned. The dragon took one look at her companion's expression and wrapped her arms about her, hugging her tightly. She stood behind Raine, still embracing her.

"I saw the white dragon again," Raine said.

"The dragon who is not a dragon?"

"Yes," Raine replied, "I don't know what she is. But she came to me again in the forest."

"And what words of wisdom did she have for you this time?"

"They were hardly wise," Raine said sarcastically. "She told us, as in you and me, to run and hide."

"That doesn't necessarily sound unwise," Talan commented.

"Do you want to run?" Raine said, turning to look over her shoulder.

"In a way, yes," Talan admitted. "But I don't think that will help. Hel will eventually find you. And while we delay the inevitable, she'll punish Arianthem mercilessly."

"Speaking of which, did you find Hyr'rok'kin?"

"Many. There are pockets springing up everywhere, which tells me they're preparing for a massive assault."

"How soon do you think it'll happen?" Raine asked with concern.

"Not imminent," Talan said, "but soon. We found the Hyr'rok'kin threat severe enough that Kylan has gone to scout the Empty Land to make sure they're not staging there."

"Will she pass into the Veil?" Raine asked.

"I told her not to," Talan said, "she'll scout the periphery, then head north."

Raine breathed a sigh of relief. The Empty Land was bordered by The Edge of the World, great cliffs that dropped into a veiled land of strangeness that separated the mortal realm from the Underworld. Horrible creatures inhabited that strange world, monstrosities that would be dangerous even to one such as Kylan.

Talan pulled Raine close and kissed her neck. "Neither of us can escape fate, but destiny will be what we make it."

And for the moment, Raine felt safe in her lover's embrace.

CHAPTER 4

Raine rose before dawn, leaving her lover still tangled in the sheets. She went out onto the terrace to watch the rising sun. The city was quiet, still recovering in slumber from the festivities that would shortly resume. One of the Queen's attendants brought her a steaming cup of tea which she took gratefully. She leaned against the marble banister, enjoying the peaceful solitude.

Movement on the adjacent terrace caught her eye as Skye came out and struck a similar pose. Skye's survey of her surroundings settled on Raine, and Raine motioned her over.

"You're up early," Raine commented as the attendant brought out a second cup of tea.

"Thank you," Skye said to the lovely server, who nodded graciously and wordlessly disappeared. "So are you."

Raine had dreamed of disturbing things, which had awakened her, but she did not share this with Skye. She had a feeling the young woman might have had her own disturbing dreams and turned her head sideways to look at her.

"Something on your mind?"

Skye did not answer at first, then spoke quietly. "Ingrid is still out there."

"I know."

It was Skye's turn to look sideways at Raine, wondering if Raine had sensed what she herself felt. Raine confirmed this.

"Idonea said the sorceress was casting a spell of binding on you when she arrived. She was able to block it, but I wonder if the smallest part did not get through."

Skye nodded in agreement. "I think it did. I feel a faint connection to her, nothing as powerful as my connection to you, but something."

"I feel it as well," Raine said.

Skye grew even more troubled. She had not thought about it from that angle. Years ago, Raine had created a bond between them to save Skye's life and keep her from passing into the Underworld. If Skye was connected to the sorceress, that meant Raine was, too.

Raine read her expression and shook her head. "The bond I created with you was physical; the one between you and Ingrid is magical. It can't affect me. I'm more concerned that she can find you."

"She found me easily enough before," Skye said. "And it's not as if she doesn't know where I am. I'm not powerful enough to defeat her, not yet. So, I'm going to have to find another way to deal with her."

"It's not as if you'll have to deal with her alone."

"I don't want to keep endangering everyone around me because of her."

"What is it she wants from you?" Raine asked.

Skye was thoughtful. "At first, I think she just wanted revenge on my great-grandfather. Now I feel like something has shifted. I know she enjoys having sex with me," she added wryly.

Raine hid a smile. The young Tavinter spoke almost matter-of-factly, tossing out a phrase that she would have choked on a few years back. She was becoming more like the Ha'kan every day.

"And I think she drinks my blood," Skye said.

"That's how she stays young."

"'Tis an odd beauty regimen," Skye remarked. "But it works."

Raine remained silent. If Skye sensed a shift in the sorceress, Raine sensed an interesting shift in Skye as well. The hazel-eyed beauty turned to her.

"You've known Ingrid a long time and had many run-ins with her. Is she evil?"

"Not exactly. She has the potential to do incredibly evil things because she's ruthless in getting what she wants. She's vain, narcissistic, and craves power. That said, she's not unnecessarily cruel, but coldly efficient. Except when it comes to getting back at Isleif. Then she's evil."

"Did she kill my father?"

"No," Raine said, shaking her head, "that was the Garmlain."

Skye appeared relieved, and was silent for a moment. "What happened between her and Isleif?"

Raine sighed. "Ingrid was very much in love with Isleif, but I don't know that he was in love with her. He had secretly pined for Tova, your great-grandmother, for years. When Tova's husband died, Isleif 'comforted' your great-grandmother, and your grandfather, Isolde's father, was the result of that affair."

"Did Tova and Isleif stay together?"

"No," Raine said. "Their affair was brief. Ingrid never knew it, but Tova broke Isleif's heart as surely as he broke hers. When Tova realized she was with child, she wasn't certain if Isleif or her husband was the father, and to her it didn't matter. She ignored the speculation and raised the boy, and soon the speculation died away. Isleif took to protecting the Tavinter from a distance, so I think he always believed the boy was his. When Isolde was born, he was certain. Her power was unmistakable."

"So, the power didn't manifest in my grandfather, but it did in my mother."

"Yes. And now it manifests in you," Raine said.

Skye was quiet while her thoughts circled back to her original rumination. "So Isleif broke Ingrid's heart."

"Yes, undoubtedly. And he's regretted it his entire life. I think at first his regret was for the consequences, her quest for revenge, but as time passed, I think he genuinely regretted the pain he caused her." Raine looked closely at Skye. "I know how compassionate you are, Skye, but don't let that compassion blind you to how dangerous she is. Don't underestimate her."

"It's not that," Skye said, brushing her hair from her eyes. "I know more than anyone what she's capable of. There just has to be a better way of dealing with her."

Raine continued to examine Skye closely. "All right," she said at last, "if you figure something out, I'll support you."

CHAPTER 5

"Now as powerful as the invisibility spell is," Idonea said to Skye, "it's a passive ability. We need to add some attack skills to your repertoire."

Today's lessons were taking place in an inner courtyard, and were attended by Gimle, Kara, and Runa. Raine was also present, but she was sprawled beneath a tree some distance away, watching sleepily through half-closed eyes. The sunlight in the small courtyard made it pleasantly warm.

Skye was dubious. "Didn't you say I should only use light magic?"

"Yes, and most destructive spells are dark magic, either full or in part. But there are a few that are purely light magic."

Kara diligently wrote down this information. Although she herself would never be able to use it, its historical and academic value to the Ha'kan was unquestioned.

"Most destructive spells are very easy for me," Idonea said. She raised her hand and cast a ball of flame at one of the straw dummies that had been placed for the lesson. It burst into flame. Before the fire could get out of control, she raised her other hand and cast a stream of pure ice. The dummy froze solid. She then swirled her hand in the air, brought a green smoky vortex to life, then thrust it toward the frozen dummy. It shattered.

"What was that last one?" Gimle asked, intrigued.

"A little something I learned from Y'arren," Idonea said. "It's more magic from the natural world than destructive, a kind of sonic tornado beyond our hearing. It uses sound to break things apart."

"Fascinating."

"If we're to keep your gift pure," Idonea said, returning to Skye, "you can't use any of these spells."

"Darn," Skye said, disappointed. The fire spell always impressed her, and that green vortex was fabulous.

"But there's a spell that can give you versions of all three of these things."

"A single spell?"

"Yes, let me show you."

Idonea held out her hand, palm up. Contrary to her usual practice, she exhibited great concentration. This caught Raine's attention, for normally Idonea flung fire and ice around as if it were nothing; that meant the spell was difficult. Idonea placed her other hand a few inches above the first, palm down, as if she were holding an invisible ball. A sphere of white light appeared between her hands, glowing hypnotically.

"Come here," Idonea said, and Skye obeyed. "Don't touch the light, but put your hands close to it."

"It's cold," Skye said in wonder.

"Yes," Idonea replied, "and feel it now."

"Now it's hot!" Skye exclaimed.

"Yes, and feel it now."

"It has a strange thrumming to it," Skye said, "a vibration."

"Exactly," Idonea said, and she released the spell. The ball of light disappeared. "I won't do much more with it because it's very difficult for me. But I think you'll do it very well."

"Better than you?" Skye said. "I doubt that."

"This is another spell of pure light magic. One that plays to your strengths. Even if you were to take up dark magic, you would never match my ability. But Isleif believes that in light magic, you may be unsurpassed."

"If you say so," Skye said, trying hard to sound convinced.

"Just try it," Idonea encouraged. "Hold your hands like this and think of holding a ball of light."

Skye copied Idonea's motions and the Ha'kan scholars held their breath as Skye concentrated. Nothing happened.

"You're thinking too much again," Idonea chided. "Close your eyes and feel the sun on your face."

Skye followed her direction.

"Now think about that light that's falling on your skin."

Skye did so, her shoulders relaxing.

"Now put that light between your hands."

Runa stifled a gasp as a marble-sized ball of light appeared, floating between Skye's hands.

"Open your eyes slowly," Idonea said, "and keep your body relaxed."

Skye opened her eyes and stared in wonder at the small light sphere.

"Breathe in, then breathe out, and let it expand a little."

The ball of light grew until it was about the size Idonea's had been.

"Good, good," Idonea said encouragingly, "now the light is a little yellowish, that means it's not pure. Try to focus and keep breathing."

Skye again followed the soothing directions and the light grew brighter and whiter.

"Now think about the light being cold, like moonlight."

Skye concentrated, but she wasn't certain if it was having the desired effect because the light felt the same to her. Idonea waved her hand near the sphere.

"Colder," she instructed, and Skye tried to obey. Idonea plucked a leaf from a nearby tree and held it next to the ball of light. Frost crept over the green surface, freezing the leaf solid.

"Now think about it humming, as if singing a song to you."

Skye smiled at the analogy. She focused and could almost hear the song. Idonea plucked a dead leaf from the ground and held it near the sphere. It dissolved into dust from the vibration.

"Excellent," Idonea said, "now think about the light being hot, like a white hot poker."

Skye did so, and Idonea plucked another leaf from the tree and held it close to the sphere. This one curled and smoked, then burst into flames.

"Wonderful!" Idonea exclaimed. "Now I want you to try something that I didn't show you. I want you to make the ball float towards the practice dummy."

"Okay," Skye said, steeling herself. She wasn't certain how to get the ball of light moving, but imagery and gestures often helped, so she blew on the ball as if blowing seeds from a dandelion. The ball of light left her hand and began to float across the courtyard towards the dummy.

"Marvelous," Idonea said, watching the ball travel to its target. When it reached the dummy, its heat was so intense it burned a perfectly round hole in the straw figure as it drifted through. Skye was ecstatic, but then a look of consternation passed over her features as the ball of light continued to drift. It reached a full-size tree and bored the same perfect hole in the trunk without slowing down. It was now headed towards the castle wall.

"Um...," Skye said.

"You can't stop it, can you?" Idonea said, her tone understated for the disaster that was unfolding. The ball of light could drill its way wall-by-wall through the entire castle, incinerating everything in its path.

"No," Skye said, aghast at what she had unleashed.

"Raine?" Idonea said.

"Already on it," Raine said.

And she was, having risen and already jogging towards the slow-moving missile. Right before it reached the wall, she reached out and grabbed it, an act that would have incinerated anyone else who tried. But upon her touch, the ball of light just sparked, then fizzled out.

"I'm so sorry," Skye said.

"I'm pretty sure that was Idonea's fault," Raine called out.

"Thank you for pointing out the obvious," Idonea called back. "There's no need to apologize," she said to Skye. "You just learned a spell that took me weeks to absorb. You might want to make sure Raine is around, though, when you practice."

"And you might want to practice that one in an open field," Gimle suggested.

"That's a very good idea," Skye said, still wide-eyed at the near disaster. But Idonea was unmoved and Raine as cheerful as ever, so she started breathing again.

"Why don't you youngsters run along," Idonea said, "I'd like a word with the First Scholar and Raine."

A relieved Skye joined Runa and Kara and they left.

"Well that was impressive," Gimle said when the three were gone.

"I'm not sure what's more impressive," Idonea said, "that the girl learns these spells so effortlessly or that she's so unconscious of her own talent."

"I remember a young mage who accompanied me on a quest years ago," Raine said, "one filled with dark magic who made up ingenious spells off the top of her head."

"I was not as humble as Skye," Idonea said.

"No," Raine said, kissing her daughter-in-law on the cheek, "you were not. But you were just as talented."

"Skye's magic is different," Idonea mused, "I have many rivals when it comes to dark magic, but light magic is its own entity, and I know no one who practices it exclusively. Speaking of practice," Idonea said, turning to Gimle, "I'm returning to the imperial capital, so you'll have to take over Skye's tutelage in the short-term. See that she practices and doesn't spend all her time on the archery range."

"I will gladly do so," Gimle said. "Although until she learns to control that spell," she continued, eying the two, singed holes, "We'll stay out of the bedroom."

"A wise decision," Idonea said, laughing, and the First Scholar left them.

"So, you'll meet us in imperial territory?" Raine asked.

"Yes. I'm only going ahead because the Baroness of Fireside has many duties of diplomacy."

"As does the daughter of a dragon," Raine said shrewdly. "Why do I feel this particular direction came from your mother?"

"Because you know her. I believe her exact words were, 'why don't you go fuck that Knight Commander of yours so that we stay in the good graces of the empire?'"

"Yes," Raine said, laughing, "that sounds exactly like her."

CHAPTER 6

Skye was wandering through the castle. The sprawling structure still confused her, and she had yet to discover every hall and room, so occasionally she just set out to explore. She was somewhere near the Queen's forum, in a series of rooms with paintings, sculptures, and statuary. The figures and busts were of beautiful women in magnificent and imposing poses. Skye lingered to read the various accounts of Ha'kan history that accompanied the artwork. The room was empty save for two of the Royal Guard, and the hall was quiet.

The clang of swords caught Skye's attention and she glanced to the Royal Guard, but they showed no reaction. Clearly the sound was not unexpected, and as laughter drifted in with the swordplay, Skye grew curious. She did not think there was any part of the castle she was forbidden, so she nodded to the two Guards as she followed the sound.

She came into a large, high-ceiling room where light streamed through enormous windows. The room was occupied by four women, and Skye stared at the unlikely scene. Astrid and Helena sat together on a bench watching the combatants and enjoying the show. Senta was using both a sword and a shield against a formidable opponent, one who also used a sword and shield in a skillful manner. Skye watched the contest, dumbfounded, for she had never seen Senta train with this particular individual.

It was the Queen.

Halla was dressed in training armor, much like Dallan's. It was light-weight leather, slightly modified with the royal insignia. It fit the Queen a bit more snugly in places, and because she was not wearing a chest plate, the swell of her breasts was pressed against the top of the leather jerkin. Skye's attention was occupied by the sheen of perspiration on those soft mounds, but only briefly as she was drawn back to the skill of the participants. Senta attacked and the Queen parried the flurry of thrusts and swings, moving backward with expert footwork. She moved in an arc, which put Senta facing the doorway, and directly facing Skye. Senta paused, lowering her sword.

It took Skye a moment to grasp that Senta was looking at her, a grin on her handsome features, while Skye stood there gaping, mouth open. And then the Queen was also regarding at her, that same knowing look on her lovely face.

"I beg your pardon, your Majesty," Skye stammered, blushing. "I didn't mean to interrupt."

"You're not interrupting, Skye," Halla said, "Although I don't know whether to be pleased or insulted by the look of shock on your face."

Skye clamped her mouth shut as both Astrid and Helena laughed. Skye tried to redeem herself.

"I—, I never thought—." Finally, Skye gathered her wits about her. "I guess I've never seen you fight before."

"No," the Queen said, laughingly calling Skye's bluff, "You didn't think I could."

"Well," Skye mumbled, "that might have been part of it."

Halla swung the sword with a fluid motion. "I once had a vocation, what did you think I was?"

"A priestess," Skye admitted before she could stop herself.

"Thank you for the compliment," Halla said, tossing a wicked glance over her shoulder to her High Priestess. "But I was of the Warrior caste before I became Queen. Would you care to spar with me?"

"What?"

Skye's befuddlement was so humorous to Senta she could not resist. "Here, take my sword. When the Queen asks you to spar, it's not a request."

Skye stepped into the room and took the sword from Senta. She took a stance and numbly raised her sword.

"Be careful," Senta warned, "she's a devious opponent."

That became apparent as the Queen lunged forward and Skye nearly went for the feint, barely recovering to block the real attack. Skye parried several thrusts and even managed a riposte. Her numbness was dissipating. Yes, she was training with the Queen of the Ha'kan, who wore the leather armor quite unlike any warrior Skye had ever seen, her lovely breasts a continual distraction. But Skye's love of battle was coming into play, overcoming her awe and consternation of her opponent. And it was apparent the Queen was enjoying the battle as well, for Skye was an opponent who required more speed and dexterity than the average training partner. Their battle was pitched and lengthy, the passion intensified when the Queen would lock swords with the young Tavinter, pressing against her as a playful diversion, then laughingly pushing her away.

The skirmish was heated in many ways, and the spectators enjoyed that heat as much as the participants. At first, Senta watched the technique of the two with a critical eye. But when there was little to critique, she settled between the two Priestesses and took the flask of water that Helena offered.

"I should warn you, your Majesty," she called out, "Skye has remarkable endurance."

Skye blushed at the innuendo while the Queen took advantage of her distraction and pressed forward. Senta grinned, knowing she could fluster the Tavinter.

"And Skye, I should warn you that the Queen can outlast even me."

Skye's blush deepened, for this inference was even less veiled than the first.

"Not always," Halla said, performing a brilliant combination that Skye barely defended against, "but I have my moments."

The fight continued, as did Senta's playful taunts, and finally it was too much for Skye. She stepped backward, out of range of the Queen's sword, and dropped her weapon. "Enough!" She said, holding her hands up in mock surrender. "I yield!"

"Ah," Senta said with relish, "I think I see a training deficiency."

"Well," Skye muttered, "As I will never stand against the Ha'kan again, 'tis an acceptable weakness."

The Queen sheathed her weapon, her bosom heaving with exertion, and Skye sought to look anywhere but at Dallan's mother. Her eyes settled on Astrid, which was worse, for the High Priestess looked at Skye with a combination of gentle sympathy and amusement. Skye bowed quickly to the three on the bench, then to the Queen.

"Forgive me, your Majesty, I—, I have to go train." She stopped, trying to gather her muddled thoughts, then just gave up. "Elsewhere."

The women were kind enough to control their laughter until Skye had scurried from the room and was out of earshot.

"That was arousing," Helena commented. "I should watch swordplay more often."

Senta took Helena by the hand. "I was a bit hard on Skye. She's fun to toy with because otherwise she's a daunting opponent."

"You were merciless," Astrid said, kissing, then patting Senta on the cheek. The High Priestess joined the Queen as the First General left with Helena on her arm.

Astrid handed Halla a towel to wipe the sweat from her brow.

"What?" the Queen asked at her knowing expression.

"You're inching towards that finish line, aren't you?"

The Queen laughed, not a bit put off by the observation. As far as she was concerned, it was only a matter of time before the girl shared her bed.

"As are you, my love," Halla replied, an allegation that Astrid did not deny, either.

Lifa moved about her Ministry quarters, softly humming to herself. Freya and Ama, members of Lifa's inner circle, sat on cushions and discussed the sexual development of several of their charges, comparing notes and making suggestions. Lifa smiled at the conversation, for the comments were gentle and loving, and once again convinced her she had chosen her staff wisely.

Leya, Freya's twin, came in and was escorting a visitor. This was an honored guest, as was evident by the fact that Freya and Ama leaped to their feet, and Lifa's entire countenance beamed her pleasure.

"Sable!" Lifa exclaimed and went to hug the woman.

Sable embraced Lifa and Lifa held her hands, stepping back to look at her.

"You're beautiful as always," Lifa said.

And Sable was beautiful. Beautiful and unique for the Ha'kan. Although the majority of Ha'kan were dark-haired, there were many color variations such as Lifa's auburn hair or Gimle's blonde hair. What was largely consistent was that the Ha'kan were all fair-skinned, the warriors being slightly sun-burnished due to their time outdoors.

But Sable's skin was ebony, a variation that was highly unusual and prized within Ha'kan society. Sable's mother possessed the same dark skin, but her grandmother was as fair as could be. The scholars had researched the phenomenon, but none had discovered the cause, and in the end, they determined the variation was simply a gift from Sjöfn. Sable's mother had never felt the sting of prejudice and had been treated the same as any other Ha'kan from birth, becoming a Scholar upon her graduation from the Academy. Her research was prized, and she had even collaborated with the First Scholar on several projects. When her daughter was born with the same lovely skin, the Ha'kan rejoiced, and when her daughter came of age and chose the vocation of Priestess, they rejoiced even more.

Lifa had approached Sable with the offer to join her staff, for the young woman was but a few years older than Lifa and was well-respected as a Priestess. But Sable had declined, and Lifa secretly worried that Sable feared she would be a "novelty." Although the Ha'kan appreciated cultural diversity, they were a remarkably homogenous race in terms of appearance.

"Have you given any more thought to joining us?" Ama asked, hope in her voice.

"I think of it all the time," Sable replied. "But that's not why I'm here. I came because I heard that you and I have something in common," she said, addressing Lifa.

Lifa was curious; she and Sable had a multitude of things in common. Although slightly apart in age, they had attended some of the same schools at the same time growing up. They shared a vocation. Their mothers were close friends. She couldn't guess what Sable was getting at, although the gleam in Sable's eye gave her a sudden insight and her eyes drifted down to Sable's stomach.

"Are you—?" Lifa asked, not daring to hope.

"I am!" Sable exclaimed. "I had suspected but didn't want to say anything until I was sure. And now it's been confirmed!"

Lifa hugged Sable tightly, and released her only so that Leya, Freya, and Ama could also share their joy with embraces. When the prolonged hugging was finished, Lifa settled onto the couch with Sable and the other priestesses settled around the cushioned circle.

"Although we'll rejoice in the birth of your child regardless, I confess I hope she has your skin," Ama said, "it's so lovely."

"Thank you," Sable said. "But as often as I've thought about joining you here in the capital, I don't want the choice to be based on a superficial characteristic."

"Do you think I would offer you the position based on your skin alone?" Lifa said, gently chiding. "Your merits as a Priestess are well known. Besides," Lifa said, glancing up the figure coming through the door, "we already have a bit of the exotic around here."

The young woman coming through the door was exquisite, slender build, olive skin, hazel eyes, light blonde hair. She looked nothing like the Ha'kan and had a very perplexed look on her face.

"Oh," Skye said, embarrassed that she had barged in, "I'm sorry Lifa, I didn't realize you had company."

Lifa laughed merrily, as did all the Priestesses as Sable looked on in wonder at Skye. "You're always welcome, silly, you know that."

Skye had a touch of color in her cheeks as she presented herself to the newcomer. She bowed in a formal manner and extended her hand, which Sable took, utterly charmed by her manner.

"Sable," Lifa said, "this is Skye."

"Ah," Sable said, "you're the Tavinter."

"I'm very pleased to meet you," Skye said.

"And I'm very pleased to meet you," Sable said. And indeed, she was, for the greeting she received held not the faintest trace of acknowledgement of the color of her skin, and Sable was not certain the Tavinter had even noticed.

Lifa was also aware of Skye's nonchalance, something that all the Ha'kan tried to maintain around Sable and her mother. Lifa particularly was sensitive to Sable's feelings. Although not singled out to the degree that Sable was, Lifa had been designated as the future High Priestess from a very young age, and sometimes constant attention, even positive, could be wearing. She could not imagine what Sable experienced. But Skye's people were much more varied in appearance, and some had skin as dark as Sable's, so Skye's indifference was genuine.

Skye sprawled onto the couch across from Lifa, a look of consternation on her face.

"And what is that look for, my little Tavinter?"

"Why didn't you tell me the Queen was a warrior?"

Lifa was baffled, both at the question and why Skye came to her as opposed to Dallan. "I guess I assumed you knew. It's no secret that the Queen was of the Warrior caste before she gave up her vocation to be Queen."

Skye continued to brood and Lifa still did not understand why. "And how is it you learned she was a warrior?" she delicately prodded.

"We just sparred."

All the Priestesses subtly shifted their positions as understanding took hold. Swordplay amongst the Ha'kan was always about more than mere training. Lifa suppressed a smile.

"And did you win?"

Skye frowned. "That's a contest you cannot win."

Sable covered her mouth, also trying to hide her smile.

"By the gods," Skye said, thinking of the last hour, "you should see her in that training armor."

Lifa could contain herself no longer and burst out laughing. "The Queen is gorgeous, why are you so troubled by that?"

"It feels wrong, or like it should be wrong," Skye asked uncertainly, "I mean, that's Dallan's mother!"

Sable was puzzled by the comment, and Lifa patted her on the thigh. "You have to remember. Skye's been with us for years, but she's not Ha'kan. No," she continued, addressing Skye, "there's nothing in the world wrong with your attraction to her. Or to the High Priestess."

Skye turned bright red. "Is it that obvious?"

"Well...," Lifa said.

Skye buried her head in her hands, then got a hold of herself. "It's not like anything would actually happen," she muttered.

"Well....," Lifa said again.

"Now that's a look on your face I don't think I've seen since the Academy," Dallan said, strolling into the room. "One I've sorely missed. And how has Lifa managed to embarrass you this time? Or perhaps it was Sable?" Dallan said, leaning down to kiss the visiting Priestess.

"It was neither of us," Lifa said, "this is your mother's work."

"Really?" Dallan said, casting Skye a wicked grin. "And what did my mother do?"

"Nothing," Skye said dismissively, "we just—, we just sparred."

"You sparred with my mother?" Dallan exclaimed. "Oh, you're in trouble now."

Dallan's laughing response told Skye the trouble would come from the Queen, not her, and it was exactly the trouble Lifa alluded to.

"Shut up," Skye said crossly, "are we going to hunt or what?"

"Rika awaits, as does Raine."

"Good," Skye said, leaping to her feet. She bowed to the Priestesses as a whole. "If you will excuse me."

"Goodbye, Skye," Lifa said, gaiety still in her voice.

Dallan clapped an arm around Skye's shoulders as they departed, and her voice drifted back.

"So, did you 'spar' with Astrid as well?"

"Oh, just shut up."

Dallan rode out the city gates, her merriment still evident. And much to Skye's discomfiture, Rika now shared in that merriment as Dallan had straightaway told her of Skye's sparring session. And when Skye confessed that she had told the Queen she thought she might have been a priestess, they both broke into uproarious laughter.

Raine rode alongside the Tavinter, sympathetic to her discomposure.

"You've done well adapting to the Ha'kan. It must be confusing sometimes."

"Don't get me wrong," Skye said, "I adore them. I wouldn't change anything in the world, except the times when I've been apart from them. But yes, sometimes it's confusing." Skye stared at the strong backs of the two women in front of them. "And I love it when Talan flusters Dallan. It somewhat evens the score."

"Talan's not much for socializing, but I'll tell her to arrange more chance meetings."

Skye's eyes glowed at the thought. "That would be wonderful."

The four rode along in comfort. An outing by the Princess would normally require accompaniment by the Royal Guard, but the presence of the Scinterian changed that. The Princess was able to take care of herself, and there was nothing the Scinterian could not handle.

They reached the edge of the forest and a Tavinter scout materialized out of the foliage. She wordlessly took the reins of the horses, signing to Skye that she would stay with the animals while the hunters continued on foot.

Skye took one step into the trees and disappeared. Both Rika and Dallan shook their heads at the feat. The Tavinter were stealth itself and Skye was like a ghost. She was probably right next to them as they set out beneath the canopy of leaves. Raine drifted off to the right and soon she, too, had disappeared. Neither Rika nor Dallan were concerned. Skye's people were probably all around them.

Which is what Skye thought, too, but strangely she did not sense anyone near her. This did not worry her; it was just unusual. Her people shadowed her constantly, never very far from their beloved leader. In truth, she had hoped to see some of them as she had spent most of her time of late in the Ha'kan capital. But it didn't seem that anyone was close to her.

So, she just enjoyed the forest. The smell of pine, the soft needles beneath her feet, the soft padding of the animals around her, the gentle buzz of insects, the various songs of the birds in the boughs above, all were a comfort and a joy to her.

And then, everything went silent. Skye stopped, unmoving, her ears straining the forest around her. Her eyes scanned the trees in front of her, then to the sides. Slowly, she turned around without making a sound.

"Hello, little one."

Directly behind her, only feet away, stood a coldly beautiful woman with long white hair and alabaster skin dressed in a white gown that was incongruous in the forest. Incongruous or not, it pushed her full breasts upward, emphasized her small waist, and clung to curvaceous hips, and Skye, as imperiled as she was at the moment, let her eyes linger in appreciation.

"Ah, I see you missed me," the sorceress said, pleased.

"Parts of you," Skye said, and Ingrid was taken aback at the admission. The girl had not moved or made any motion to flee, but Ingrid warned her, nonetheless.

"Don't attempt your spells," she said, "the ones that allowed you to escape last time. My spell of binding captured enough of you that you won't be able to hide."

Skye wasn't certain that was true. As powerful as the sorceress was, the ephemeral spell, by design, was impenetrable. Still, she had no urge to test that theory.

"What do you want from me?" Skye asked.

This gave the sorceress pause. What a ridiculous question. What did the girl think she wanted from her? She had kidnapped her twice, the first time brutalizing her, the second time deceiving her into believing they were lovers. She had threatened her life and the lives of her friends. She had sworn vengeance on her and her entire family.

But the power of that question was haunting, because for the first time, as Ingrid stood in the forest, ready to strike down the girl in front of her, she wasn't certain.

"Because," Skye continued casually, "if it's revenge against Isleif, that incentive is almost gone. My great-grandfather is not long for this world, and soon he'll know nothing of any pain you exact from me."

Ingrid tried to ignore the logic of those words. She tried to convince herself that it would be enough for her to know that she was hurting Isleif's offspring. She tried, and she failed. Her great joy was to feel the wizard's pain, but he would feel nothing when he was dead.

"So again, I must ask you, what is it you want from me?"

"I want your blood, and I want you in my bed."

The statement was blunt and brutal, meant to shock and offend. But it had little effect on the Tavinter, who merely considered the words.

"There are ways other than force that could be achieved."

This stunned the sorceress into complete silence. The girl she had ripped from the center of a Ha'kan encampment years before had transitioned into something inexplicable.

"I don't think you want to be in a 'relationship,'" Skye continued, musing aloud, "if I remember rightly, you got bored very quickly with 'Signe.'"

"Yes," Ingrid said mockingly, "I must say I prefer you as yourself. And the day-to-day living was something of a yawn."

"So then, I have a proposal for you."

Ingrid's disbelief was now complete. That the girl would stand here so calmly and make an offer to her sworn enemy was incomprehensible. And the offer itself was even more incomprehensible.

"I will come to you on every full moon and stay with you a night and a day. You may do with me as you wish during that time, but all other times you will leave me and mine alone."

Ingrid repeated the proposal slowly, enunciating every word. "You would give yourself up to me, allow me to do anything I want, every month, for the rest of your life?"

"I would," Skye said, then shrugged her shoulders. "I enjoy having sex with you."

This again stunned the sorceress into silence. She narrowed her eyes. "And you would give me your blood?"

"Within reason, yes," Skye said. "You can't threaten my life, but based on past experience, you don't need much."

"And your friends would allow you to abide by such a pact?"

Dallan and Rika stepped from the forest, their swords drawn. Then, they very deliberately sheathed the weapons.

"We would," Dallan said. She turned to Skye. "This is consensual and of your own free will?"

Skye nodded.

"How in the world can this be of your own free will?" Ingrid asked, her incredulity causing her to argue against her own interests.

"Because Raine could have killed you at any time."

And it was then that Ingrid felt the twin pricks of the blades at her sides. The Scinterian stood right behind her, both swords hovering within inches of her heart. The deadly warrior had moved in silently and stood poised, the most dangerous creature in the world to a sorceress: one completely immune to magic.

Raine, too, sheathed her swords and stepped around the dazed woman.

"Is this truly your wish, Skye?"

"It is."

Raine turned to Ingrid. "And will you abide by the terms of this agreement?"

Ingrid shook her head, not in a negative response but in disbelief. She looked to Dallan and Rika. "And you two would approve of this?"

They seemed almost confused by the question. "Of course, we would," Dallan said, "it's a perfectly reasonable solution."

And only then did Ingrid truly grasp the nature of the Ha'kan. Many thought they understood the communal race and their emphasis on sexuality, but most were interpreting it through the prism of their own reality. The Ha'kan handled everything through sex, not just what was pleasurable, but conflict, disagreement, and hostility as well. The social mores that others attempted to lay over the Ha'kan culture were not only inapplicable, they were diametrically opposed. There was no jealousy or possessiveness or anger in the mind of the Princess of the Ha'kan, she merely saw Skye's proposal as a viable resolution. Granted, Dallan's anger at the sorceress was such she gladly would have killed her, but if Skye wanted another solution, Dallan would abide by her wishes.

"And you would allow this?" Ingrid said, turning to the Scinterian.

"I will on one condition," Raine said. "You must have no more contact with the Goddess of the Underworld."

"Hel has no further use of me," Ingrid said bitterly, "and has abandoned my cause."

"Hel has only her own cause." Raine said. "Trust me, you're better off."

Ingrid turned to Skye. "So, you'll come to me in seven days' time? And stay from moonrise to moonrise?"

"I will," Skye declared solemnly.

"Then I accept your proposal, and we will see."

"Do you trust her?" Weynild asked Raine.

Raine shifted her head, which was lying on Weynild's shoulder. Her fine features were accentuated by the moonlight streaming through the window.

"Not entirely. But I reminded her before she left that I can find her as easily as she can find Skye and warned her she has but a single chance. I think she got the message."

Weynild chuckled. "I'm sure she did. You can be very persuasive."

"As can you. And I believe the thought of us coming after her together will dissuade her from hurting or abducting Skye." Raine toyed with Weynild's silver hair. "And Skye has her own forms of persuasion."

"Yes, that Tavinter becomes more like the Ha'kan every day. Other than concern for her safety, no one appears to object to the terms of the pact itself."

"As Dallan pointed out, it's a very Ha'kan solution. I think it would have been better just to kill Ingrid, but that wasn't Skye's wish."

Weynild rolled over on top of Raine, her amber eyes glowing. "It wasn't your wish, either. You've had many opportunities to kill Ingrid in her lifetime, and yet you never did so."

"And she had many opportunities to kill Skye, and never did so. I think I felt a little sorry for Ingrid," Raine said, "that must be the Arlanian in me. It's rare that it overcomes my Scinterian half."

"I like it when it does," Weynild said, leaning down to kiss her.

CHAPTER 7

I t was with great trepidation the Ha'kan said goodbye to Skye when the full moon rose. Skye assured them that she would see them the next day, but the pact that had seemed so logical in theory now seemed fraught with peril when the terms were due. Raine rode out with Skye alone and waited with her in the forest at the agreed upon location.

"Are you sure you want to do this?" Raine asked.

"Yes," Skye said, "I think this will work."

Raine examined the youngster, who was an adult woman now, but still a child to her. Skye was nervous, but there was also an air of anticipation about her. Perhaps it was not merely the Ha'kan influence that had driven Skye to take this path; the Tavinter reckless love of adventure could be in play as well.

A disturbance in the air in front of them drew their attention, and a swirling mass of multi-colored light threw the trees around them into stark relief. The portal opened and the sorceress stepped through, and even Raine looked upon her with appreciation. She had dressed for the occasion and wore a stunning red gown that set off all her attributes.

"I must say I'm surprised you're here."

"The Tavinter always keep their word," Skye said.

"And I'll remind you of your word, Ingrid," Raine said. "I've spared your life many times. But if Skye isn't returned to me tomorrow, at this time, unharmed, I'll hunt you down. And my mercy will end."

A challenge such as this, uttered by anyone but the Scinterian, would have been greeted with contempt by Ingrid. But she responded with only mild irritation.

"I gave my word, Scinterian. And unless you wish to take the Tavinter's place, I suggest you step back."

"If I took her place," Raine said, "we would both be hunted down by a dragon, a fate I wouldn't wish upon either of us."

Raine stepped back and Skye stepped forward. Ingrid held her hand out and Skye took it, and together they stepped through the still-open portal and disappeared.

"I hope you know what you're doing," Raine murmured to the empty forest.

"That was amazing," Skye said breathlessly when they reappeared.

"You've never traveled through a portal?"

"No, Idonea said it was dangerous."

"Hmm," Ingrid said. It certainly would be dangerous for this girl to travel through unaccompanied. The sorceress had learned how to protect herself from the creatures that resided in the netherworld, at least those on the periphery that she skirted through. But this one emanated light magic, a beacon that would draw all sorts of demonic beings. She would have to remember that in the future.

"If" she took her back, Ingrid thought to herself. She still couldn't quite believe the girl was here and that she had come willingly. It was the ultimate act of naiveté on her part, to give herself up to her enemy, and she couldn't believe the Scinterian had bought into it, despite all her threats.

Skye glanced around the luxuriously furnished room. They were in some type of tower, the round stone walls indicating it was a very large structure. It was cool, but a fire burned in the hearth, giving off a welcome heat. Skye moved to the fireplace and rubbed her hands in the warmth.

"So, what did you want to do first?" she asked, trying to keep her voice steady.

The sorceress sensed the trepidation and it pleased her. The constant confidence the girl displayed was unnerving.

"I think I'm thirsty."

Skye swallowed hard. "Very well." She started to roll up her sleeve, then paused. "Unless you want to drink directly—?"

This was the strangest conversation the sorceress had ever had. "I'm not a vampyre," she said, "I'll use the doctor's equipment."

She brought out the thin needle, the long tube, and the glass jar. At the last minute, she set the glass jar down and lifted a jewel-encrusted goblet. "I guess I don't need that, anymore."

No, Skye thought, the doctor's subterfuge was no longer needed. This was no medical procedure designed to keep her docile. She sat down in the cushioned chair, wincing only slightly as the sorceress inserted the needle into the vein on her arm. The blood snaked through the tubing and into the goblet, and Skye watched the life pour out of her, wondering if the sorceress would stop when the goblet was full.

She did. She clamped the tubing, removed the needle from Skye's arm, then drained the last of the red liquid from the tube into the chalice. She pressed her hand on the wound, murmured a single word, and when she removed the hand, the wound was gone.

"Thank you," Skye said, startled by the feat.

"Don't be too impressed," Ingrid said dryly. "That's the extent of my healing abilities."

She started to sit down, then caught herself. "I'm being remiss as a hostess." She poured Skye a glass of wine, then settled across from her in front of the fire, goblet in hand.

"To our agreement," the sorceress said, and took a long drink from the chalice.

Skye took a sip of the wine. She was already feeling a little light-headed from the loss of blood, and her tolerance for spirits was very low. Rika teased her about it constantly. The thought of Rika brought an immense homesickness that tightened her chest and throat. She pushed the feelings away and concentrated on the sorceress, who was clearly enjoying her drink. She really was a lovely woman, harshly beautiful angular features, a long, slender neck that transitioned into the softness of her breasts. The breasts seemed to swim before Skye's eyes, the softness blurring, then coming into focus once more. She looked at the wine glass.

"You didn't have to do that," she said.

Ingrid finished her drink and stood. "I don't completely trust you," she said as she took Skye's hand and got her to her feet.

"*You* don't trust *me*?" Skye said in disbelief.

Ingrid led her to the bed and pushed her backward. The girl offered no resistance, but that might not have been voluntary given her loss of blood and the drug she had been given. It was one of Ingrid's favorite concoctions, rendering the victim almost helpless but with no loss of consciousness or sensation. It was also one she had given Skye before, on many occasions.

For this reason, Skye was none too concerned. She recognized the feeling of lassitude, the wonderful lethargy that relaxed her beneath this woman's touch. Her clothing was gone, and that alabaster skin was pressed against her, the breasts so close to her mouth that even in her enfeebled state she was able to capture the nipple in her mouth. The woman's hips ground against her in response and she suckled harder, even lightly biting as she felt the warm wetness come forth on her torso.

And the sorceress was mad with desire. This was the same and yet so very different than before. The girl was not tricked into believing she was someone else. She knew exactly who she was, and she knew exactly who the woman was on top of her. And Ingrid was thinking less of Isleif and more of Tova, the leader of the Tavinter, the great-grandmother of the girl beneath her. Strangely, all these years, she had thought little of this woman who was an equal part in the betrayal, and with enormous excitement, it occurred to her that she was not just fucking Isleif's offspring, she was fucking the current leader of the Tavinter herself. She was bedding the beloved leader of the people she hated, and the girl would come to her willingly again-and-again. This was better than imprisoning her, better than killing her, and a more epic revenge on Tova than she ever could have imagined or orchestrated.

Skye knew nothing of these thoughts and would not have cared if she did. Something was driving the sorceress to ecstasy, so she wrapped her legs around her and simply enjoyed the ride.

A night later, Raine waited patiently in the forest, accompanied by a few of her wolf companions. She had assured the Ha'kan she would return with Skye shortly, and now she hoped that assurance was not in vain. She saw a flash of light between the trees, some distance away, and began making her way towards it. About halfway there, she met up with Skye, who was pushing her way through the thick foliage. The wolves yelped in greeting.

Raine hugged the girl tightly, then held her at arm's length. "Well, you look like you're still in one piece."

"I'm a little tired," Skye confessed, "but beyond that, I'm fine."

"And you're fine with this agreement?"

"Oh yes," Skye said, "Although I thought this might be a way to fix things, that wasn't my whole motivation. The sorceress really is fabulous in bed."

Raine grinned. "Spoken like a true Ha'kan. I've often seen them use sex as a weapon. Not by force or coercion, but by pure seduction. Now, this isn't going to turn into one of those things where Ingrid likes you a little too much and tries to keep you for other reasons?"

"I doubt that," Skye said, laughing. "I'm a plaything to her. She loves little beyond herself. And already she's begun prodding me for the secrets of my magic. She got angry when I told her I have no idea how I do the things I do, but then I think she realized I was telling the truth."

"You're a terrible liar, so that's in your favor."

"Yes, and she knows it, which is also in my favor, at least when it comes to this."

They came to the horses at the edge of the forest, held by the same silent Tavinter scout who had met them previously. She nodded to her leader, then disappeared back into the forest. Skye mounted her beast, as did Raine.

"You know," Raine said teasingly, "as the leader of the Tavinter, you could begin negotiating alliances all around Arianthem with this newfound skill of yours."

"Shut up," Skye said, turning bright red, and the Scinterian's laughter echoed across the plain.

CHAPTER 8

At long last it was time for the Queen's entourage to set out for Mount Alfheim. The partings were poignant, but the general excitement made it less so. Those traveling were looking forward to the adventure, and those remaining were looking forward to trying out their future positions.

"I am so proud of you," Queen Halla said to her daughter, caressing her cheek. "You'll make a wonderful ruler in my absence."

Senta stood in front of Rika, causing the Future First General to slightly look up as Senta was the only person present who was taller than she was. Senta clapped her hand on Rika's shoulder. "You guard the Princess," Senta said solemnly, "and the country."

"I will," Rika said, nodding just as gravely. For once, her manner was deadly serious with no joviality, but when Senta grinned, so did she.

Gimle was giving Kara some last-minute, detailed instructions on a series of research experiments which Kara was desperately trying to commit to memory. Finally, Gimle stopped herself and placed her hands on Kara's shoulders. "Use your best judgment," Gimle said, and Kara smiled.

Astrid hugged Lifa, no doubt in her mind as to her successor's success. Although Lifa's mother, Helena, would stay in the capital, it would be Lifa who was in charge of the Ministry. Her daughters Eira and Embla were also staying, as were Runa and Solvi. It would be good experience for all the younger women.

Skye was speaking with her childhood friend, Torsten.

"I wish I was going with you," he said.

"So do I," Skye admitted, "but you're my second, which means you're the First Ranger in my absence."

Torsten nodded, grinning slightly. "Who would have thought the two of us would wind up here?"

Skye thought back to the two little barbarians running through the forest, half-naked and joyously poor.

"Certainly not me."

"A large contingency will travel with you, out of sight, headed by Aeric," Torsten said, "Flynt will stay here with me."

"Good."

Dallan approached so Torsten stepped respectfully away.

"You take care of my mother," Dallan said, hugging her tightly, "and yourself."

A commotion at the city gates drew everyone's attention as two grand figures rode in on enormous horses. Raine was dressed in her Scinterian armor, her blue and gold markings visible and snaking up her forearms to her shoulders. Her chiseled features were even more striking in the early morning sunlight. Her horse was a superb gray Roan, hands taller than any horse save that of her companion's. Talan rode next to her on a huge black stallion, stately and imposing in her iridescent, fiery red armor, the light glinting off her silver hair as her amber eyes coolly assessed the waiting troop. Magnificent was the only way to describe them.

"I think we're going to be pretty safe," Skye said.

All mounted their horses and a great cheer went up in the capital as the Queen of the Ha'kan set off.

The celebratory mood remained for some time as the horses loped along. All the Ha'kan were expert on horseback: it was a required skill learned at the Academy. And because they had given themselves ample time to make the trip, it was an easy pace, allowing for much conversation and general enjoyment.

"She rides like she's a centaur," Senta said, watching Skye. The Ha'kan might have been expert equestrians, but Skye rode as if the horse were a part of her. She thought nothing of standing up on the back of her mount to pluck low-hanging fruit from the boughs above them, which she shared with the Royal Guard around her.

"Yes," Gimle said, "I saw her speaking to the horse for some time before mounting it."

"She did that even at the Academy, and was laughed at, right up until the horse did exactly what she wanted," Senta replied. "Many of the Royal Guard now speak to their horses before riding."

"Would anyone like an apple?" Skye said, riding up with fruit in both hands and guiding the horse with her knees.

Senta, Gimle, and Astrid all declined, but the Queen reached out and accepted the gift.

"Thank you, Skye," Halla said warmly, causing Skye to blush profusely and nearly fall off her horse. She wheeled around and hurriedly returned to the Royal Guard.

"A little bit of forbidden fruit?" Astrid observed.

"Hardly forbidden," Halla said, taking a bite of the apple and eliciting a chuckle from Senta.

"Raine also looks natural on a horse," Gimle commented, examining the pair that led their troop. Talan and Raine rode out ahead side-by-side, talking quietly and enjoying one another's company. The lithe, muscular Scinterian looked fabulous on the horse.

"What do you expect?" Halla said, "She's used to riding a dragon."

The double-meaning entertained the four, right up until both Raine and Talan turned around to look back at them. The dragon merely raised an eyebrow while Raine clearly found the comment funny. They returned to their conversation.

"And I forgot how acute both their hearing is," Halla said, not the least bit embarrassed. She was in a wonderful mood.

"Skye," Senta said, calling out to her. Skye trotted her horse back over and came up alongside Senta.

"Are your people around us?"

"Yes, of course. There's one right there."

Skye pointed to a tree in the nearby forest, but none of the Ha'kan saw anything. She held up her hand in that general direction and made a series of signs. What looked like a patch of moss on the side of the tree turned and signed back to Skye.

"I'll never get used to that," Senta said as the Queen and Astrid gasped in appreciation.

Skye signed again and the patch of moss faded away.

"And Raine's wolves are following us, too. Look, there's one right there."

A huge, barrel-chested black wolf, probably an alpha male, trotted from the edge of the forest and began loping alongside Raine. She leaned down to have a conversation with him. When finished, she ruffled the fur on the back of his neck and sat upright. The wolf disappeared back into the forest.

"Now the wolves obey Raine because of Fenrir, correct?" Gimle asked. It felt odd to speak so casually of the gods, but with Raine the extraordinary was commonplace.

"They don't really obey her," Skye said, "it's more like they love her and treat her like one of the pack. Really, like the head of their pack. I wonder if we'll meet Fenrir on this journey?" she mused.

"What?" Gimle exclaimed, echoed by the other three.

"I met Fenrir once, or at least I think it was him, when I was with Raine. He came to Raine as a gigantic wolf. From what I can see, they're close friends."

"Imagine that," the Queen murmured.

"And that bird up there, that's another sentinel that travels with Raine. I think she said it was one of Freyja's children."

All four women glanced up at the enormous hawk that before had gone unnoticed. It was indeed following their progress, flying ahead and then looping back on the air currents.

"How extraordinary," Gimle said.

"For someone who's immune to magic," Astrid observed, "Raine is certainly surrounded by it."

And for whatever reason, this observation made Skye very happy.

Despite their leisurely pace, the troop made good time and arrived at the locale Raine and the Tavinter had scouted for their camp long before the sun set. It was a clearing that bordered a small lake, and the tents went up rapidly, erected by the Royal Guard. Senta watched their progress with a critical eye but was pleased with the skilled construction. There was no hurry now, but a battlefield situation could require such speed, and no opportunity for training was ever passed up.

The Ha'kan carried provisions, but now Senta wondered if that was necessary, for Skye's people came out of the forest bearing all sorts of game, nuts, and berries. Skye herself wasted no time but trotted down to the lake and was soon reeling in fish. Gimle joined her and Senta looked on with a trace of envy.

"Why don't you go join them?" Halla suggested.

Senta opened her mouth to articulate all the reasons why she couldn't, then snapped her jaw shut. The camp was set up; the perimeter was secure. They had enough food for twice their number on a journey twice as long. The Tavinter had scouted the surrounding area for miles. There was a dragon and a Scinterian leaning casually against a tree at the edge of the clearing.

"Perhaps I will," Senta said, then headed down to the shore.

The Queen watched her stern General jog to the lake with a youthful enthusiasm she had not seen Senta display in years.

"And why is it we don't do this more often?" Halla asked Astrid.

Astrid was seated in a comfortable lounge chair before the makeshift fire pit the Royal Guard had constructed out of stones.

"I have no idea," Astrid said as Halla sat down beside her. "The fresh air is invigorating."

Halla's eyes drifted across the campsite to settle on Raine and Talan. "Those two are amazing."

Astrid turned to the pair, who sat apart from the general assembly. Although the Ha'kan had often seen them together, it was rare to see them in such an intimate and unaffected manner. The silver-haired woman ran her fingers through Raine's hair, and the adoration that Raine felt for the dragon was unmistakable. The violet in her eyes was apparent even from a distance. And the fact that the Scinterian treated the dragon so playfully was extraordinary since Talan was a creature that inspired nothing but terror in most.

"They are indeed."

One of the Royal Guard approached Raine and stopped a respectful distance away. Raine acknowledged her with a tilt of her head.

"Do you wish us to set up a tent for you?"

"No, thank you," Raine said, "we prefer to sleep in the open."

"As you wish," the Guard said, and bowed as she stepped away. The First Ranger had expressed the same desire.

"Speaking of which," Talan said, "I should go hunt before it gets any darker."

"Are you sure you're not going on patrol?" Raine asked teasingly.

"I'll keep my eyes open for Hyr'rok'kin, but I trust the Tavinter scouts. No, I could consume the entire trip's provisions in a single sitting, and I doubt there are enough fish in that lake to fill me."

"Ah, that's true," Raine said, getting to her feet. She gallantly extended her hand to help the woman who needed none and pulled Talan upright. The two walked to the far side of the lake. Talan leaned down to kiss Raine, then the two separated. The woman in the fiery red armor disappeared in a flash of yellow light, and an enormous fiery red dragon appeared in her place. The dragon took two great steps and was airborne. Talan had purposely moved some distance away as the great wind generated by those mighty wings would have knocked the tents to the ground and undone all the Royal Guard's hard work in an instant.

The entire encampment had stopped as one to take in the sight of the dragon, but things returned to normal as Raine strolled back to the camp. She brushed the dust and grass from her breeches, then joined the Queen and High Priestess at the fire pit.

"Is Talan going somewhere?" Halla asked.

"She's just going to get a bite to eat," Raine said.

"But we have so much food here."

"She eats, um, a lot."

"Oh," Halla said delicately, "of course."

"You don't like to be away from her," Astrid said, observing the subtle change in Raine's demeanor.

"I would stay by her side constantly if I could," Raine said, "but in truth, we're never apart."

The words caused Halla to look closer at the Scinterian. It was a superbly romantic declaration, but also something more, as if it held some deeper truth about their relationship.

"Look what I caught!"

Skye came up with a string of large fish, which she proudly displayed. Senta and Gimle followed, each also bearing a string of fish.

"Skye's fish seem to be much larger than yours, First General," Astrid said.

Senta took the good-natured teasing as intended. "I will defer to my First Ranger in just about any wilderness skill. Besides," Senta said with a wicked glance at the High Priestess, "size isn't everything."

"A lesson I had some difficulty teaching her years ago," Astrid said to Halla.

"Perhaps I was deliberately slow because I was enjoying the lessons," Senta said.

Raine enjoyed the conversation of the Ha'kan. There was a constant, sensual undertone that could flare into overt sexuality at any moment. It was playful but unobtrusive, sensuous, but not excessive. And even Talan had found the Queen's earlier comment about "riding the dragon" humorous, although she had been quick to point out that it was generally the dragon who rode her.

The evening meal was consumed with relish, and the campsite settled into quiet contentment. Muted conversations mixed with the buzz of insects, the hoot of owls, the howl of wolves, and the various stirrings of night creatures. All went to bed early with full stomachs and a delicious tiredness.

Halla was drifting off to sleep, her head on Astrid's shoulder, when Senta came through the flap of the tent. She put her hand gently on the Queen's arm.

"Is something wrong?

"No," Senta said quietly, "we're very safe. There's just something I wanted you to see."

Halla and Astrid stepped gingerly from the tent, barefoot. The Tavinter were sleeping on bedrolls about the campfire. Skye's bedroll was empty because she stood staring at something in the clearing, her slender form outlined in the moonlight. Gimle stood next to her, and Astrid and Halla joined them.

"By the gods," Halla murmured.

Talan'alaith'illaria, Queen of all Dragons, lay in the clearing at the edge of lake, taking up a vast amount of space and blocking out half the night sky. She was peacefully sleeping, wings tucked, her long tail stretched out and her massive head curled about so it rested next to her stomach. The great body rose with every slow breath, then fell with every exhalation.

And tucked between her head and her stomach was a beautiful woman, a woman who slept soundly despite rising and falling with every prodigious breath, despite being surrounded with sharp, jagged spikes, despite the potential of being crushed by that colossal weight. She had an arm draped over the bony, plated ridge of the dragon's brow, unconcerned for the world around her. The woman slept the deep sleep of someone completely safe, completely comfortable, and completely loved.

The Ha'kan were deeply moved by the sight, and it stayed with them, even in their dreams, the rest of the night.

CHAPTER 9

The troop continued to make good time and travel without incident to the imperial border. The Ha'kan had notified the imperials of their intent to travel through their land and been granted ingress, but Raine had not expected to be greeted by anyone. She shielded her eyes from the sun as she examined the cloud of dust approaching them. The Tavinter had not sounded the alarm, so she was not particularly worried.

It was an imperial troop, all heavily armored and impressively armed. At the head of the troop was a large woman with fair hair and ruddy features, attractive in a rough-hewn sort of way. Her expression was normally stern and had worn lines into her face, but when she smiled, those lines disappeared, and she was surprisingly good-looking. She was smiling now.

"Knight Commander," Raine said in greeting.

"Raine," Nerthus said. She nodded to Talan. "Your Majesty," she said with deference.

Nerthus was rarely polite to anyone, so the courtesy and respect of this greeting was significant. Talan was petrifying in her natural form, but to Nerthus her human form was even more intimidating. The silver-haired woman could deliver a look of such disdain it shriveled all in her path. Nerthus had more than once been the target of such a stare.

Idonea rode up beside Nerthus. "We were going to meet you further on, but this was the Emperor's idea."

"How so?" Senta asked, leading her horse next to Raine's. The Queen had also come forward, and Nerthus bowed from the waist, still on her mount. The men behind her were surreptitiously trying to get a look at the Ha'kan.

"Your Majesty," Nerthus said again.

"Knight Commander," Halla responded.

"The Emperor has traveled ahead," Idonea continued, "he may already be in elven territory. It's so rare that anyone is granted access to their land, I think he's taking advantage of the opportunity."

"But he wanted to honor you with an escort," Nerthus said. "And the Baroness as well."

Talan snorted.

"Don't believe I deserve the honor?" Idonea said, feigning insult.

"I don't believe you need the protection," Talan said.

"Thank you, mother." She examined the stallion that Talan was sitting on, then leaned over and slapped it on the flank. "Nice horse."

"We're grateful to you," Queen Halla said to Nerthus, "and if we don't require your protection, we'll certainly enjoy your company."

"Thank you, your Majesty."

The imperial troops fell in behind the Ha'kan procession. Talan and Raine still led, and Idonea joined them. Nerthus and her second in command were slightly behind them. Senta rode up beside the Knight Commander.

"Did you ever think you would see such a convoy through your lands?"

Nerthus was grateful for the First General's interaction. The Ha'kan were all a bit overwhelming.

"No, I never would have even dreamed of such a thing."

And her men were in complete agreement. Although they had been hand-picked, chosen for their professionalism, experience and presentation, they all were fighting not to look like starry-eyed youth. The Ha'kan were extraordinary, and the stories that revolved around the all-female race did not do them justice. They were as beautiful as everyone said, but they were much larger than imagined, and imposing. Those that had dismissed accounts of their proficiency in battle revised their opinions. The Queen and her Royal Staff were wrapped in sensuality, so gorgeous it was hard not to stare. The slender Tavinter was like an ethereal sprite, a young forest goddess, and when her people slipped in and out of the forest, it was astonishing.

And then there was the dragon and the Scinterian, which really, there were no words for. And when wolves joined their procession, the men knew that this was a story they would tell for generations.

The troop ambled on peacefully. The Royal Guard engaged the imperial troops in conversation, and soon they were talking of battles and strategy, weapons and tactics, all the interests of warriors since the beginning of time.

Skye entertained the Queen and High Priestess with the tales of her people, and Gimle was impressed with the detail that Skye recounted from memory. Skye had initially been a poor student at the Academy, but when Kara had discovered that Skye learned best by hearing, Skye went to the top of her class. The Tavinter had few written records and passed down their history through an oral tradition, so Skye's ability to memorize was phenomenal.

Idonea inched up between Raine and Talan.

"So, do you have any fears of an attack at the Ceremony?"

"Of course," Talan said, "Every leader of Arianthem will be there. But I also fear an attack in our absence." She nodded to the sky. "I have my sentries out as well."

Idonea looked up and at first did not see anything. Then the dark speck moved between her and the sun, and she focused on the object. It was flying far too high to be a bird.

"The dragons are out," Idonea said.

"Yes," Talan confirmed. "They scour the land for signs of Hyr'rok'kin, but they're also looking for Volva."

"That bitch," Idonea said, "I'd like to choke the life from her."

Talan glanced to her daughter. Most who dared threaten an Ancient Dragon would draw only laughter from her, but Idonea had grown strong, and she was proud of the girl.

"Not if I get to her first," Raine said darkly, and the blue and gold markings rose on her forearms.

"Well," Talan said, "hopefully we'll all get to kill her together, like one big happy family."

In two days' travel, they came to the edge of the Deep Woods. They would make a short detour into the forest before they would return to the main highway and begin to head upward towards Mount Alfheim. Talan left them, taking to the skies, and Raine led the troop onward. Both the Ha'kan and the imperials were glad for the presence of the Tavinter. They moved through the forest unerringly at a dizzying pace.

Skye signed to an apparently empty patch of forest, and her scout confirmed what she already sensed.

Raine had sensed it as well. "The wood elves?"

"Yes," Skye said, "they've made contact up there and will join us soon."

"Good."

And true to the scout's report, it was not long before a group of elves appeared in the woods ahead of them. Raine dismounted and spoke to their leader, a tall, fair-haired male who spoke to Raine in Elvish.

"Well met, Scinterian."

"Cool in summer and warmth in winter," Raine said, delivering the traditional greeting of the wood elves.

The wood elves were notoriously reclusive and not demonstrative, so it was with some surprise the imperials watched the elf embrace the Scinterian. The affection of the wood elves for the warrior was evident.

"She doesn't have an enemy in the world," Nerthus noted.

"Not in this world," Idonea said, and Nerthus bit her tongue.

Raine continued on foot, talking quietly with the elf while the horses behind picked their way through the thick forest. The sounds of an encampment began to drift to them on the gentle breeze. Livestock was bleating, there was the clang of a hammer on metal, and as they got closer, the murmur of voices could be heard.

The wood elves stopped as one as the large procession came into the clearing. Raine approached Senta and Nerthus.

"They say you can set up camp over there," Raine said, waving to an area just east of the camp.

"Raine!"

A curvaceous, auburn-haired woman approached on the arm of a slim, dark-haired wood elf.

"Dagna," Raine exclaimed, "Elyara!"

The three women embraced, and Dagna held Raine at arm's length. "Let me look at you. You look as young as ever."

"Even the elves age faster than Raine," Elyara said.

Both Dagna and Elyara had accompanied Raine on her quest to the Underworld decades before and had been attached to one another ever since.

But Dagna appeared much older than both of them as humans aged much faster than the other races of Arianthem.

"And how is the Bard of the Imperial Realm?" Raine asked, using Dagna's official title.

"Fabulous," Dagna said, "and as Bard I've been granted access to the Ceremony of Assumption so that I may record the event for posterity's sake."

"Excellent," Raine said, "so you'll be coming with us?"

"Yes," Elyara said, "and I'll be going as well."

"Let me guess, you'll be representing Y'arren."

"Yes. A great honor for me since I'm not of her clan by birth. But she doesn't want to leave our lands during this time."

"As much as I'll miss her on the journey," Raine said, "in a way I'm glad she's staying behind."

Elyara glanced over at Skye, who was engaging with a few of the elves. She lowered her voice. "And Isleif is failing fast. I don't think Y'arren will leave his side until he passes from this world."

"I'm glad Skye will get to see him."

"It may be the last time she sees him," Elyara said sadly. She caught herself. "Enough of that. This is a time for celebration. The wood elves have never entertained the Ha'kan before."

Queen Halla approached on the arm of Senta. Both Elyara and Dagna bowed deeply.

"Hello, Elyara, Dagna," the Queen said kindly.

"Your Majesty," they replied in unison.

Raine proffered her arm to the Queen, and she and Senta made the exchange. Raine escorted her through the throngs of wood elves who peered at the lovely woman with circumspect curiosity. Raine and the Queen approached a tiny, wizened old elf who stood at the bottom of a staircase between two pillars. She had startling green eyes and wore a green cloak embroidered with the symbols of nature's magic.

"Queen Halla," Raine said, "may I introduce you to Y'arren, matriarch of the wood elves."

The Queen gave a deep curtesy to Y'arren, and a pleased murmur swept through the throng of elves at the sign of respect from the powerful leader. Y'arren solemnly returned the bow, then her face broke into a beatific smile that illuminated her face.

"So formal, my goddaughter," she said to Raine, then addressed the Queen. "I see where your daughter gets her grace."

"Thank you," Halla said.

Y'arren reached out her hand and the Queen took it, then the two began to walk up the stairs together. Raine smiled at the sight, the tall, elegant leader of the Ha'kan and the tiny wood elf walking and comfortably holding hands.

"We have so enjoyed the tea and sweets you sent," Y'arren said, her voice drifting back. "Those sugared biscuits are divine..."

Raine went to help Senta and Nerthus set up camp, which was hardly necessary because between the Tavinter and the wood elves, the Royal Guard and imperials were overwhelmed with assistance. Idonea joined Elyara and Dagna in front of one of the outdoor fire pits, and they fell to talking about old times. Once Nerthus was finished with her duties, she hovered about them.

"Oh, for gods' sake, join us," Idonea said.

"Thank you," Nerthus said gruffly, and sat down. Dagna was fairly astonished at the change in Nerthus. The Knight Commander had been a cold, arrogant woman, insulting, particularly to mages whom she considered dangerous and possibly even immoral. She had looked down her nose at

Dagna for being a bard and at Elyara for being both an elf and a mage. Raine she had looked at with disdain, thinking her nothing more than a mercenary. Once her eyes were opened, she was chagrined to learn that Raine was "the Raine" from the legend, and that both Elyara and Dagna had accompanied her on that epic quest to the Underworld. And when Nerthus met Idonea, a mage swirling with the dark magic she hated, she had fallen hard, and everything had changed.

Idonea turned back to Elyara. "So how is my master?"

"He fades," Elyara said sadly, "I think he was waiting to see Skye one last time."

Skye walked into Y'arren's cave, taking a moment to let her eyes adjust to the dim lighting. The Queen, High Priestess, and First Scholar sat around the fire pit, three stylish and graceful women perfectly at home in the rustic surroundings. The scene made Skye smile. Her eyes searched the room, but the hand on her sleeve gave away the location of whom she was looking for. She turned to the frail, gray-bearded man, for the first time eye-to-eye as she had grown and he had shrunk. She had tears in her eyes as she hugged him tightly.

"Now, now, my little sparrow," he said, wiping the tears from her eyes, "let's have none of that. Why don't we go for a walk? It's been a long time since I've been outside."

"Are you sure you should?" Skye asked. He was weak, fragile even, and she didn't want to tire him out.

"I'll lean on you," he said, and Y'arren watched the two go, not with sadness, but with a sense of the inevitable.

Skye helped her great-grandfather carefully down the steps, and all the elves who passed nodded with deference. Idonea noted from a distance that Isleif was weaker than she had ever seen him.

Still, his step was light as he moved through the trees, enjoying the sunlight with the love of his life. Out of all the things that he had accomplished in his long lifetime, the magical creature next to him was truly the best.

"So," Isleif said, "word has it that you've chosen to deal with Ingrid in a most unique manner."

Skye grinned and Isleif marveled at the change in her. The youngster he had handed over to the Ha'kan years ago would have blushed dark red and been speechless, unable to even stammer out a reply. Nor would she have ever decided on such a course of action.

"I decided to handle it in the Ha'kan way, which I think caught her completely off-guard."

"I'm sure it did," Isleif said, chuckling. He grew serious. "I regretted my actions with Ingrid. At first, because I feared her retaliation on the ones I loved. But later I felt a different responsibility. I feared I had created the dark creature she had become."

The young woman shook her head. "People make their own choices. No one decides for them. Raine taught me that, that destiny is something you make, not something that's thrust upon you."

"Raine said that?" Isleif said thoughtfully.

"She did," Skye said. "Ingrid had many choices, and she chose a path of evil and revenge. Now maybe she can choose a different path."

"She's always going to be wicked," Isleif warned.

"I know that," Skye said, the grin returning. "I don't mind it so much in certain circumstances."

"Oh, by the gods, you're so much like me sometimes," the wizard said, and the two walked arm-in-arm through the forest.

It was late in the evening and most of the camp had gone to bed. Raine stood at the top of the stairs, leaning against a pillar, staring out at the horizon lost in thought.

"And are you hiding from me?"

"Of course not," Raine said, acknowledging Y'arren's presence, affection in her tone. "You were very busy with the Ha'kan and the imperials. It's not often the wood elves host a head of state."

"The Ha'kan are a most gracious and elegant people," Y'arren said, "the imperials?" She shrugged her shoulders and made a dismissive noise. "They're growing on me."

Raine let out a deep breath, almost a sigh, and Y'arren looked at her shrewdly.

"You hide your mood from the others, but you cannot hide it from me."

"I know that," Raine said. "I feel—"

She paused, looking for words that would explain the oppressive weight she had felt for weeks.

"I feel like events are closing in on me. Like time is running out."

"The prophecy will be fulfilled," Y'arren said.

"But it's so obscure," Raine said, "And we still don't know the final line."

"The Dragon's Lover, felled by the closest of allies, carries into death without dying that which saves all worlds," Y'arren quoted. "I think the 'saves all worlds' is what you should hold close."

"I saw the white dragon again," Raine said. "She told me that this prophecy was given to Hel."

This sobered Y'arren. This she had not known.

"You saw the white dragon again?"

"I did. She came to me in the forest. She told me that Hel knows the final line."

Y'arren considered this, and all its implications. She could see into the future, but the future was always unclear.

"Tell me what you see," Raine said urgently, placing her hands on her godmother's shoulders.

"Your time is near," Y'arren said, her green eyes glowing in the night. "And you will go into the darkness. I cannot see to the end of it, but I know that your victory hinges on embracing what you think is your greatest weakness."

Raine's jaw clenched, for she knew exactly what Y'arren was talking about, and the matriarch confirmed it.

"It is the gifts of your mother's people that will decide your fate."

The troop spent another day and night in the wood elf encampment, but soon it was time to leave. The parting was poignant, especially the farewells to Isleif. Raine embraced the wizard she had known for over a century, and he planted a kiss as a blessing on her forehead. Idonea had to brush away a tear as she said farewell to her master of two decades, grateful that she had been able to spend this last time with him. And when Skye hugged her great-grandfather, many openly sobbed. But Skye, with the resolve the Tavinter were known for, squared her shoulders, and only the shininess of her eyes betrayed the tears that were held there.

"You've made me so proud, little sparrow. Continue your training with Idonea. I left her much instruction for you."

Skye nodded, swallowing hard. "And that one," he said, indicating Raine, "you follow that one wherever she goes, even through the Gates of Hel itself."

"I will," Skye promised.

Just then, a hot wind blew through the trees and leaves scattered as a colossal red dragon swooped low over the tree tops. The massive creature let out a deafening roar, scattering animals in the underbrush, a farewell from the Queen of all Dragons to the greatest wizard that Arianthem had ever known. Isleif waved his staff at the tribute, and the dragon wheeled about and disappeared over the horizon.

Hearts were heavy as the band set out, and both Raine and Skye remained on foot, silently trodding next to one another. There were murmured snippets of conversation but, by and large, the group was quiet. Finally, Raine could bear the oppressive mood no more.

"Do you see that rock up there, the one beyond the tree line?" Raine asked.

Skye squinted off in the distance. "Yes, I see it."

"I'll race you to it.

CHAPTER 10

The land began to change. To the north, Mount Alfheim rose up out of the mists in all of its glory. To the east, the Deep Woods fell away. To the south, the bulk of the empire stretched out. But to the west was a barren land, one that was as forbidding as its name. Raine sat upon the black stallion that had been Talan's steed and gazed out at the vast desert

"So, this is the Empty Land," Senta said.

"Yes. It's a land of nothingness, and almost nothing survives in it. Insects, scarabs, a few snakes, but little else."

"And you crossed over this land?" Nerthus said.

"Yes," Raine replied, "and Idonea, Dagna, and Elyara were with me. As was Feyden, the brother of Maeva, and Lorifal of the dwarves. And Bristol, of course. There was another with us, Gunnar, but he passed away not long ago. He never recovered from the touch of the Membrane."

"That was the creature that touched you," Senta said, "that monster that was in the castle courtyard when you rescued us from the Reapers."

"Yes," Raine said, the muscle in her jaw working. The Membrane was an abomination created by Hel, a fusion of mouths, limbs, breasts, and sexual organs of those cursed by the Goddess of Death. The monstrosity perpetually pleasured itself and was in a constant, painful orgasm. It had a particular affinity for Raine. "On our quest, it touched Idonea as well."

Idonea came up beside Raine, the sight of the bleak landscape evoking memories in her, also. "You saved me. You drew it away by revealing your eyes. That was the first time that Hel saw you."

There was a trace of self-recrimination in Idonea's voice, a kind of tacit recognition that Hel had discovered Raine because of her.

"I'm guessing Hel would have found me sooner or later," Raine said, dismissing Idonea's guilt, "given her past relationship with your mother."

"And what's beyond the Empty Land?" Gimle asked, deeply interested.

"The Veil," Raine replied. "The Empty Land drops off at The Edge of the World, cliffs so high you can't see the bottom. And when you work your way down, you go into the Veil."

"What is the Veil like?" Skye asked, and Elyara shivered.

"It's a horrible place," Raine said. "The miasma that separates the mortal realm from the Underworld. It's full of demons and wraiths, strange plants that can attack you, and many, many Reapers."

"It felt like it took us years to get through it," Dagna said.

"Indeed," Raine said, also lost in the recollection. "And once through, it only gets worse. Then you come upon the first set of Gates, which lead into the red and black courtyard, which seems to stretch on forever. And then you come to the Gates of Hel themselves."

"They were enormous," Idonea recalled. "With Hel's visage on them."

"And they were being held open by the Scales of Light and Dark," Elyara added.

"Yes, which my love destroyed," Raine said.

The Ha'kan were all holding their breaths as the women recounted the tale they had heard a thousand times, yet never quite like this.

"And then you killed the dragon, Ragnar," Skye prompted, for she had read the poem at the Sjöfn Academy and committed it to memory.

"Yes," Raine said a wry grin on her face. "He was going to take Idonea's soul and thought me easy prey, right up until he realized I was a Scinterian. I reminded him that the Scinterians were dragon slayers long before they became the dragons' allies."

"That was probably the best moment of all," Dagna said.

"The look on his face...." Elyara agreed.

The four were silent for a moment.

"And then we closed the gate," Raine said, as if it were no matter, "and we didn't see the Hyr'rok'kin again for almost two decades."

"Raine," Skye said uncertainly, "what's that?"

Skye's tone of voice caught Raine's attention and she looked out across the Empty Land. "It looks like dust," she said, frowning. There shouldn't be anything in the Empty Land to kick up dust. She signaled her raptor in the sky, and the great hawk set out across the desert. A shadow fell over them as something blocked out the sun. The red dragon, which was never far from them, had also seen the cloud of dust. Talan was not far behind the hawk, flying to inspect the disturbance.

All sat tensely in their saddles, awaiting report. The dust cloud, although still very far away, was getting larger.

"Talan won't engage by herself, will she?" Senta asked.

"No," Raine said, "she would have picked me up if she meant to fight. She's just scouting right now."

Raine's voice was calm, but there was an underlying intensity that Senta recognized. She was preparing for battle.

"Knight Commander? Do you have any troops stationed near here?"

Nerthus rode up abreast of Raine. "We have garrisons all along the Empty Land. But they're sparsely staffed, more of sentry stations with light defensive capabilities."

"Do you think those are Hyr'rok'kin?" Senta asked.

"I do," Raine replied. "The desert plays tricks with the eyes, but they are still some ways off. We have a few hours. Send some of your troops to the nearest strongholds," she said, directing Nerthus, "have them bring back anyone they can." With a wave, Nerthus dispatched the soldiers who rode off at breakneck speed. "How many of the Royal Guard are here?" Raine asked.

"Just over fifty," Senta said.

"You would stand with us? Fight on imperial soil?" Nerthus asked.

"Of course, we would," the Queen said, riding up. "My First General and my Battle Mage," she said with a nod to Gimle, "are at your disposal." She looked down at her gown. "I'm going to go change."

Raine mentally calculated the distance and the size of the approaching force and looked around her. Sixty or so of the Ha'kan, the same number of imperials.

"Skye, how many of your people are here?"

Skye signaled into the air for general assembly, and Tavinter began appearing everywhere. Despite the lack of cover, they still had managed to travel almost undetected.

"We're about thirty in number," Aeric said, having been close enough to hear Raine.

"Good," Raine said.

"Raine," Senta said uncertainly, "I can't judge this distance as well as you, but that force must be in the thousands."

"Yes," Raine said, "and maybe in the tens of thousands. This is the largest force I've seen since we shut the gates."

"Do you think we can stand against such numbers?"

"I've seen these odds before," Raine said, "and we were but eight. Three of those that stood with me then are here with me now."

Idonea, Dagna, and Elyara stared resolutely out at the approaching horde. They had been here before, led into an impossible battle, hopelessly outnumbered. Yet they had been led into battle by a Scinterian who lived and breathed to fight, the same one who stood before them now.

"Gimle," Raine ordered, "your strength is your wards. Begin preparing defensive capabilities against arrows, spears, any projectiles. Idonea," she said to the raven-haired mage, "I'm going to need you and Elyara to use your imagination."

"This is going to be fun," Idonea said, and Skye marveled at her cool demeanor. Skye did not fear battle: she had spent three years at war and the Tavinter had been greatly outnumbered. But she had faced the Ha'kan, not Hyr'rok'kin, and she did not think the Hyr'rok'kin would exhibit the same restraint as her former enemy. No, this would be a fight to the death.

"Idonea," Raine began, "didn't your mother say she had a sentry over the Empty Land?"

"She did."

"Well, I wonder what happened to it," Raine said with the beginnings of concern. Talan had been gone for some time, and although the distance was vast, the dragon could have covered it by now. She shielded her eyes, frustrated that she could not see. A speck was approaching, and Raine viewed its approach with hope. But it was too small to be a dragon.

The huge raptor swept down and landed in front of Raine. The bird was so large it stood nearly taller than Raine. Its wing was bloodied, and feathers were torn near the wound.

"You're hurt!" Raine exclaimed.

Elyara came over and pressed her hand to the wound while the bird communicated with a series of screeches and flaps with its good wing. Raine listened intently, her expression darkening.

"There's some type of winged Hyr'rok'kin," she said, "something I've not seen or heard of before." She turned to Idonea. "Talan's in trouble."

With two steps, Raine reached the huge black stallion and leaped upon its back. The horse reared and tossed its head as Raine spun it around. "Stay here!" she cried.

Many started to mount their horses to follow her, but Idonea held up her hand, restraining them with a spell.

"She'll bring Talan back," Idonea said firmly. "Stand fast."

Skye chafed at the restraint. "She'll never get there in time! I wish we had another dragon."

"We do," Idonea said calmly.

And as Raine rode out, leaning low on the horse's back, the legs of the horse churning and the hooves flashing, they continued to gain speed. The horse was traveling at an impossible pace, the black flanks heaving, and somehow still gaining velocity. Then, with a brilliant flash of red light, the beast dissolved and Raine was no longer on a horse, but was riding a dragon. The black dragon skimmed low to the ground, then with two great thrusts of his wings he went airborne, high into the sky where he caught a thermal updraft and shot even more skyward.

"Drakar was with us the whole time?" Skye asked.

"Oh yes," Idonea said, "probably in heaven being ridden by both my mother and Raine."

"I had all these witty comments to make," Drakar said, looking back over his long neck at Raine, "but I've quite forgotten them all."

"I'm sure they'll come back to you when we've rescued your mother."

"It's hard to picture my mother needing help," Drakar said.

And yet she did. Even from a distance, they could see that the great creature was bedeviled by many smaller, flying creatures. They weren't quite bat or bird, but some disgusting combination of the two, with the same leathery and pus-like qualities of all the Hyr'rok'kin.

"Why doesn't she flee?" Drakar asked.

"She can't," Raine said.

And then Drakar saw it, the rope about one of Talan's legs, the golden rope held in the claws of some of the bat-like creatures. Talan strained against it, fighting the whole time against the monsters that dove in to tear and slice at the flesh of the beautiful drake.

"If what my mother said is true, there's nothing I can do against that rope."

That was so, Raine thought. Talan had been restrained by a mere filament before, and it had drained her strength to near death. Hel had designed the cable to restrain dragons.

"I can't disenchant it, either," Raine said. "But I can kill whatever's on the other end of it."

Drakar swooped down and in and under in an acrobatic maneuver. With a sharp twist of her wrist, Raine snapped out her bow and began firing arrows with the powerful weapon. They caught the flying Hyr'rok'kin by surprise, for they had been told there was not another dragon in the vicinity once they killed the sentry and captured the red one. The black dragon incinerated a trio of them while the Scinterian took down two more with her deadly arrows. Drakar swooped in tightly to Talan, knocking one free that clung with its fangs buried in her wing. In the close quarters, Raine moved to her swords, slicing up whatever Drakar veered towards that somehow escaped his flame.

Talan was now more free to defend herself, but two of the bat-like creatures still held the rope. Drakar had to steer clear of the dangerous cord, uncertain what effect its touch would have on him. But Raine had no fear of the golden thread. On one precarious dive, she leaped from Drakar's neck and grabbed hold of the taut line, sliding down its length towards the two monstrosities that held her love in check. She met them feet first, hitting one with such force it knocked it free and sent it spinning toward the ground.

The other she fought one-handed, blocking the vicious swipes of its talons with her short sword. With a tremendous swing, she decapitated the beast.

But now that the line was no longer held taut, Raine hurtled toward the ground. The rope snapped tight in a jarring move, and yet somehow, she managed to hold on. Now she was only a few feet off the ground and able to get a very good look at the multitude of Hyr'rok'kin that gnashed their teeth below her, leaping up and slicing their claws at her.

Talan did her best to gain altitude as Raine began to climb the rope. The muscles of her arms corded and flexed as she pulled herself upward with incredible strength. She finally reached the great toes of the dragon's foot and pulled herself onto the foot, wrapping an arm about the ankle. With the other, she struggled to jar the heavy rope loose, angered when she saw where it had cut into the skin. With a pull, she freed the ankle and the rope went tumbling down in a spiral. It hit the ground below, knocking a group of Shards off their feet.

Instantly, Talan's strength returned.

"Drakar, we must retreat!"

The black dragon blew one last funnel of fire, then swept his wings forward and wheeled about. He joined his mother in their head-long flight back across the Empty Land.

Raine clung to Talan, caressing the smooth, scaled skin between the heavy plates. She leaned down and pressed her lips to the skin, devastated that Talan had been injured.

"I'm fine, little one," Talan said.

"How were they able to get that rope around you?"

"I didn't see it at first. They shot it from the ground with some sort of catapult. And then those flying monsters attacked me and I wasn't able to get myself free."

"I've never seen flying Hyr'rok'kin before," Raine said.

"Nor I," Talan said grimly. "I'm certain they were bred specifically with dragons in mind."

That made sense, Raine thought. Air superiority was no longer guaranteed. It would not be so easy for the dragons to annihilate the ground troops if they were fighting their own battle in the air.

The sight of both dragons returning was a huge relief to those waiting at the edge of the Empty Land. Talan and Drakar both landed, and once Raine was free of the dragon's neck, they transformed to their human shapes. Raine ran to Talan and embraced her tightly. It was unusual for Talan to ever be in any danger, let alone injured, and it grieved Raine. Idonea ran to her brother and hugged him, and he took advantage and pressed against her in a lingering manner.

"That's enough," Talan said to her children. Drakar released his sister with a look of disappointment.

"Elyara," Raine said, supporting Talan when she started to limp. "Could you see to Talan's wound?"

"Of course," the doe-eyed elf said, and moved to tend the injury with her gentle touch. Gimle also moved to assist.

"What happened?" Senta asked.

"We have a few problems," Raine said as everyone gathered around. "I got a very good look at them up close, and there are thousands of them. Worse, they have some sort of flying Shard with them that will have to be dealt with or the dragons will take a lot of damage. The flying beasts weren't heavily armored, like Talan or Drakar, but they were fast. In a swarm, and in a multitude, they could take down a lesser dragon."

"But neither Talan or Drakar is a lesser dragon," Senta pointed out.

"No, but the Hyr'rok'kin have something else with them. A rope that can restrain even an Ancient Dragon, and it's huge. That's what caused the injury to Talan. They fired one from a catapult and it caught her ankle in flight. She's lucky she didn't go down."

"Is it the same—?" Idonea asked.

"Yes, it's the same."

Idonea frowned, her dark eyebrows knitting together. Her mother had been incapacitated by little more than a strand of that material and it had taken all of Idonea's power to break her free. A rope, especially one the size that Raine was describing, would be impossible to break. And it could very well kill her mother if it drained her like before.

"We're going to have to take out those catapults," Senta said grimly.

"Right," Raine said.

"This is not good territory to fight in," Nerthus said "especially so out-numbered."

The Knight Commander, First General, and Scinterian all looked out at the flat plain stretching before them. It was terrible terrain to fight in. There was no cover, it was wide-open, and the much larger force could easily flank them on both sides. They would be hemmed in, and if they couldn't make it back to the Deep Woods, they would be surrounded.

"Yes," Raine agreed, "Terrible. Which is why we're going to change it. Elyara, can you do it?"

"I can," the slender elf said with confidence.

"Do you want it to move this time?" Idonea asked, leaving Senta and Nerthus baffled.

"No," Raine replied. "You can decorate it with your usual touch, but I need you to save your power for something else."

Raine knelt down and began to draw figures in the sand. All leaned in as she began to lay out her plan. When all was said, Senta leaned back, stunned. She could barely picture what the mages were going to attempt. Overall, the situation was nigh insurmountable, but the Scinterian had just laid out a battle plan that might work. Raine's grasp of tactics and strategy was jaw-dropping. Although Senta had seen Raine fight on many occasions, she had never seen her lead before. Raine's command presence was such that it did not occur to Nerthus or Senta to take charge of the campaign.

Senta was staring out over the desert, mulling this strange acquiescence to the Scinterian's authority when Talan came up beside her.

"The plan is brilliant," Senta commented.

"You seem surprised."

"No. I guess it's that I've always seen her fight as an individual, not as part of an army. Her military leadership is extraordinary."

Talan gave a low chuckle. "You have to remember, the Scinterians didn't have Kings or Queens, they had only Generals. In the Great War, Garik Estania, Raine's father, was one of the greatest." The dragon started to walk off, then paused.

"In fact," she said over her shoulder, "if the Scinterians did have a King or an Emperor, it probably would have been him."

Before the sun reached its peak, they were joined by another seventy or so imperial troops, a welcome addition. But as the dust loomed closer and closer, the true size of the approaching horde became evident and an unease settled on the small force. The imperials shifted from side-to-side, restless. The Tavinter checked the fletching on their arrows, and then did so again. The Ha'kan stood in formation while their Queen sat on her horse in full armor, next to her First General. Astrid, like all Ha'kan, was proficient with a sword, but both Halla and Senta insisted she stay to the rear of their forces. The Queen was the soul of her people, the First General, its strong right arm, and the First Scholar, its mind. But the High Priestess was the beating heart itself, and none could bear for her to be in danger.

One stood out in front of everyone, arms crossed, serenely confident as she gazed out across the desert. Her eyes were the ice-blue color of her father. The blue and gold markings rose on her skin, a testament to a ceremony so painful most would not survive. The multitude of weapons she carried gleamed in the sunlight. If any felt their courage begin to waver, they had only to look to her and it would return. And as the mass approaching them began to resolve into clumps, then individual figures, she smiled a grim smile full of anticipation.

"Can you imagine an army of Scinterians?" Senta murmured.

As the horde approached, the Hyr'rok'kin foot soldiers began to spread out across the horizon, confirming their intent to flank the much smaller force, then surround it. Raine watched carefully for signs of Hell Hounds, the dreadful four-legged beasts that could cover the remaining distance in an instant. She had seen some while dangling above them on the golden rope, but she did not see them now. And the winged Hyr'rok'kin hovered above their own army, waiting for their dispatch.

Raine counted nine Marrow Shards, which were easily identifiable because they were enormous and lumbered along, taking one step to their comrades forty. The size of the hideous creatures caused dismay even among the more seasoned troops.

"The first time I met Raine," Skye said quietly, "she killed one of those things single-handedly. Ran right up the side of it and cut off its head, laughing the whole time."

This recount heartened those near her, and they gripped their weapons, steeling themselves.

Elyara and Idonea joined Raine, one on each side.

"I don't see or sense any Reapers," Idonea said.

"Nor I," Elyara agreed.

"That's good," Raine said. The wraith-like monstrosities carried their own dangers above-and-beyond the Horde Shards. They required powerful magic to banish.

"Maybe they got tired of you killing them," Idonea said. A single Reaper could destroy a small town, and Raine had prevailed against them on several occasions. Her immunity to their dark magic proved a powerful, defensive weapon.

"I never get tired of killing them."

The approaching horde was now close enough that they could be heard. Their howls, screams, and screeches were unnerving. The roars of the Marrow Shards carried across on the wind. And although they could not be seen, the baying and growling of the Hell Hounds carried as well. Senta glanced to Raine because the enemy was getting very close. The very end of their line was slowly beginning to curve around to trap the small army.

Raine removed her bow from her belt and with a flick of her wrist, snapped the deadly weapon into form. She pulled an arrow from her quiver and very carefully took aim.

"What is she doing?" Queen Halla said, and Senta shook her head. They were not even close to being in range. It was twice, possibly even three times the reach of even a skilled archer. Accuracy wasn't achievable at that distance.

Raine made one adjustment for the wind, then let the arrow fly. The projectile sped away and disappeared, too small to be seen. And across that great expanse, the lead Hyr'rok'kin clutched his chest and fell to the ground, spitting blood from the arrow buried in his heart.

The horde stopped.

"Well, that got their attention," Raine said.

"By the gods," Senta muttered. That hadn't been an attack, it was a warning.

Slowly, but with far less certainty, the horde began to move forward again. They were no longer moving lockstep, however, and were far less organized. Still, the massive force began to curl around the much smaller army.

"Elyara," Raine said, "would you do the honors?"

The elven mage, Elyara of the Halvor, acolyte of Y'arren of the Deep Woods, raised her slender arms to the heavens, and the ground began to rumble. The sands began to shift and snake about like something alive. The earth shook as two great lines split the terrain and moved outward across the desert. The lines became cracks, then fissures, then the sand itself shot straight upward, becoming two enormous walls that stretched out nearly the distance to the approaching army. They were too high to scale, even for the Marrow Shards, and too thick to breach.

"Well done," Raine said as Elyara calmly maintained the spell.

"She created a canyon," Queen Halla said in disbelief.

"Perfect terrain for a small force to engage a much larger one," Senta said, now understanding Raine's intent. The Hyr'rok'kin could no longer flank them and would be forced to funnel through the narrow entrance to fight.

Nerthus also assessed the dramatic change in terrain and wondered whatever made her think that going into battle without mages was a good idea. It would have taken months, if not years to build such a siege structure.

"Would you like to add a few touches?" Raine asked.

"I would be glad to," Idonea said. At the entrance of the canyon, the sand again began to slither about. Deadly spikes shot out from the ground, pointing outward at the approaching army. That would slow any full frontal assault down the funnel, and a frontal assault was now the only option left for the Hyr'rok'kin.

The horde had again come to a halt, or at least the part that they could see. The walls blocked out all the troops that had sought to curve around, and only the force directly in front of them was visible. The foot soldiers milled about uncertainly while their superiors screamed at them in fury.

"If I know them," Raine said, "they'll send those Marrow Shards to try and take down those spikes. If they do," Raine said to Idonea, "let them fall. I need you to conserve your energy."

Raine mounted her roan and rode over to Gimle. "I'll need you to come with me." She signed to Skye, and Skye chose ten of her best archers. They mounted up and followed Raine.

"In and out," Raine cautioned. "This is just the beginning skirmish."

The troops left behind tried to quell their impatience for battle and their anxiety for their comrades. That was a very small force Raine was leading into the maw of the enemy. But Raine did not travel all the way down to the spikes.

"Is this close enough?" she asked Skye.

"Yes, this is within our range."

Raine nodded. It was what she anticipated. The skilled Tavinter were within their range, but still well out of the Hyr'rok'kin range. "Aim for their throats, here," she said, indicating her own jugular vein. "It's their weakest spot."

True to Raine's prediction, the Marrow Shards let loose their terrible roar and began stampeding toward the spiked entrance. They swung their massive fists and smashed the sharpened, earthen spears, but not without taking damage. Blood began to run from their torsos, legs, and arms, and they screamed in rage and pain. But the spikes were going down.

The Tavinter coordinated their targets without outward communication, intuitively knowing which enemy was theirs.

"Fire!" Raine said, and all loosed their arrows.

The projectiles flitted through the air, almost all finding the necks of the Marrow Shards. The lumbering beasts staggered about, clutching their throats, stumbling into one another. Three crashed to the ground, one impaled itself upon a bed of spikes, and a fifth began to crawl away, mortally wounded.

"That's enough," Raine said, "retreat!"

The small unit wheeled about and fled back down the walled canyon. As Raine expected, the flying Hyr'rok'kin massed into a swarm and gave chase. They were almost upon them.

"Gimle!" Raine called out, "a ward!"

The First Scholar concentrated, and the air above the fleeing Tavinter shimmered, then took on a more solid form, appearing almost liquid. But it was not liquid, for the bat-like creatures slammed against it as if it were a solid wall, bouncing backwards in confusion and rage. They screeched in a frenzy of indignation, denied the prey that had seemed helpless.

"I can't maintain the ward very long!"

"You don't have to!" Raine cried back.

And Gimle understood as something enormous blocked out the sun. A fiery red dragon glided over them and a blast of flame drove the flying Hyr'rok'kin backward. An ebony dragon joined in, diving downward and wreaking his own havoc. The two, heavily plated dragons sustained little damage from the sharp talons of the monstrosities.

"Not too close, Drakar," Raine murmured. Both dragons were to reveal themselves, but only over the canyon and not too close to the entrance where the enemy was massing. She wanted the Hyr'rok'kin to bring the catapults forward. Those had to be destroyed, and early in the battle. Otherwise, she would not risk Talan or Drakar.

Talan turned sharply about, but Drakar skimmed close to the fallen Marrow Shards. The red dragon roared her disapproval, and the black dragon, too, wheeled about.

The diversion of the dragons had allowed the small band that Raine led to return to the safety of their comrades, and the Ha'kan archers dissuaded any of the bat-like creatures from coming too near. They flitted about in an angry, turbulent cloud.

Raine sat on her horse out in front of her army, ignoring the occasional dive from one of the flying Hyr'rok'kin, or casually slicing it in two if it came too near. She peered down the canyon.

The foot soldiers were beginning to make their way through the opening. They were slowed by the remaining spikes and the fallen Marrow Shards, but their numbers were increasing.

"Companies, prepare!"

Nerthus sat on her horse in front of the imperial force, the largest present. Dagna sat next to her. They would march down the left side of the canyon. Senta and the Queen sat in front of the Ha'kan force, and they would march down the right. Skye and the Tavinter would provide ranged support. Elyara had raised a platform from the sand, and Idonea stood where they could look out over the battle. Gimle soon joined them.

Raine raised her arm, then sliced her hand downward, and the assembly as one began marching forward. It was an awesome sight, the steel plated armor of the imperials, the red and gold armor of the Ha'kan, the gleaming leather of the Tavinter. Raine had made the decision to forego cavalry, and now Senta understood why. Speed would not be an issue in this close confinement. Once the horses had gone forward, they would have nowhere to turn if needed, not without trampling the infantry behind them. The majority of the horses had been left behind for retreat, if it came to escape.

But that one, Senta thought, eying the Scinterian. That one was not retreating. She would die on this battlefield or kill every last Hyr'rok'kin here.

The dragons wheeled about behind them and Raine watched the entrance carefully. The wind was kicking up the sand and making it hard to see.

Their self-made canyon was creating its own weather system. But through the haze, Raine could see the massive, wheeled contraption she was looking for. The catapult was slowly being pushed and pulled through the opening by a multitude of Hyr'rok'kin. The monsters growled and gnashed their teeth as they strained from exertion.

Raine continued to scan. How many catapults were there? It was crucial they destroy them all before the dragons fully engaged. She could see a second coming in behind the first. She could even make out that deadly golden rope. This would be the most dangerous part of the battle, when they would meet the Hyr'rok'kin head on, without the help of the dragons and at the mercy of the winged miscreations.

The catapult was coming into focus now. It was heavily plated which meant it would be resistant to fire, truly a weapon designed to be used against a dragon. It might be possible to destroy it with brute force, but that would entail wading through an army of Hyr'rok'kin. There might be some spell that Elyara or Idonea could use against it, but Elyara was tasked with holding up the walls while Raine wanted Idonea to reserve her power. But there was something else they could use.

"Skye," Raine called out, dismounting her horse as Skye ran over. "Can you create one of those balls of light?"

"I think so," Skye said doubtfully.

"No thinking," Raine said, "just do it."

"All right."

Skye took a deep breath, and everything fell away. The bats dive-bombing her disappeared. Raine's casual swatting of the foul creatures seemed very distant. The army behind her was there and yet not there. She held her hands out and apart, one palm up, one palm down, as if grasping emptiness. The air began to churn between her palms and light filled the empty space. The light formed into a ball and Skye took a deep breath, focusing. In response, the light grew more intense, and as Skye began to spread her hands apart, the light grew bigger. Soon, it was near her height in diameter.

A trickle of sweat ran down her temple but she ignored it. She had been practicing on increasing the speed of her projectiles, but this one was so large, it would take monumental effort just to get it moving. She tensed her shoulders, braced herself in a stance, and pushed the ball of light outward as if she were pushing against a wall. And the huge ball of light slowly began to bob and float across the battlefield.

Skye relaxed. Once the ball was moving, the spell required no effort. It was hard to get it in motion, but she had yet to figure out how to get it to stop. Normally it would just keep going until Raine touched it.

Raine wasn't going to stop it today.

The ball of light floated across the battlefield in an almost leisurely manner, confusing the Hyr'rok'kin who stopped to look at the phenomenon. It didn't look dangerous. In fact, it looked ridiculously benign. So much so that the Shard foot soldiers began laughing, awful guffawing and croaking sounds. It floated toward them silently, gently, and the closest soldier reached out to touch it.

It incinerated his hand off. He screamed, holding the cauterized stump, but that was not enough warning for the nearest Hyr'rok'kin who stood in the ball of light's path, befuddled by their comrade's fate. The ball went through them like hot steel through butter, meeting no resistance and turning them to ash. The ball continued to float forward, unimpeded, but now the terrified Hyr'rok'kin struggled to get out of its way, pushing and shoving one another, trampling those unfortunate enough to fall. The ball didn't care; it just slowly floated through them, gently annihilating everything in its path.

Raine watched the progress of the sphere of light. Skye had good aim. The ball was heading right toward the first catapult and would likely catch the second as well. The Hyr'rok'kin superiors were screaming at those holding the chains that pulled the catapult forward, but they were panicked, haphazardly pushing and pulling in all directions so that the catapult went nowhere. As the floating ball neared, having cut a clean path through their entire force, they threw the chains to the side and fled, despite the blows and curses of their commanders.

The ball of light bobbed along, its speed and direction still constant, and as it reached the catapult, it didn't slow down. It passed right through the base of the armament, burning a perfectly round hole through the heavyweight structure. The Hyr'rok'kin stared at the burning edges of the huge hole, incredulous, then ran in terror as the colossal weapon began to collapse. Pieces of metal and wood rained down on the Hyr'rok'kin, crushing dozens as the remains toppled over.

But the ball of light wasn't finished. It still floated on in its dreamy, indifferent manner, burning everything in its path that was too slow to get out of the way. It was not directly in line with the second catapult, but it was close enough. It reached the weapon and began shaving off the entire right side, leaving a moon shaped outline that smoked and burned. Removed of its support, the second catapult swayed, then toppled to the ground with a massive thud and cloud of dust, taking many more Hyr'rok'kin with it.

The army of Ha'kan and imperials cheered.

"I wonder how long that ball will go for?" Raine said, and Skye had to laugh for the Scinterian was utterly casual.

"Maybe all the way to the Veil," she speculated. "I still don't know how to stop it."

"You're tired," Raine said, noting Skye's fatigue. "I don't want you in hand-to-hand combat. You stay back and coordinate the archers. You're going to have to keep the winged Hyr'rok'kin at bay." She leaned close. "And you stay on the Queen."

Skye nodded. Halla was insistent that she ride into battle with her troops, a possibility that wouldn't even have occurred to Skye a few months ago. It was appropriate the Queen lead with her First General at her side, but her death would be devastating to the Ha'kan, and personally devastating to Skye. Dallan would be inconsolable. Raine did not need to tell her to protect Senta and the Queen: her eyes would be on them constantly.

Now that the Hyr'rok'kin were in disarray, the slow march of the small army resumed, then picked up pace. It became a head-long charge as Raine went sailing into the front lines of the enemy, swords flashing in a whirling blur of death. The front forces of the imperials and Ha'kan clashed with the monstrosities, and Senta was pleased to see her front line hold. She dismounted to better get into the fray, as did the Queen. The Ha'kan did not have the advantage of numbers that the imperials had, but they had a very disciplined method of fighting. They maintained close ranks, fighting shoulder-to-shoulder, and as the front ranks tired, they rotated to the rear in tight coordination. The exception was the First General, who fought out front ferociously, her broad sword swinging in a huge arc that destroyed everything in its path. The Queen, too, fought up front, but she with sword and shield, dancing nimbly about and slicing here-and-there.

Senta tried to stay near the Queen, but a horde separated her. Her blood turned to ice as she saw the group of Hyr'rok'kin attempt to isolate the Ha'kan leader, knowing the value of this prey. But their attempt was in vain as a multitude of arrows flitted in, unerringly finding the throats, eyes, or hearts of the foul beasts. Senta glanced up at Skye, who along with a few of her rangers, had found a ledge on the wall. Skye smiled grimly, and Senta once again thanked the gods for the day that girl had walked into the Sjöfn Academy.

Nerthus had also been unhorsed, and now attracted the attention of a horde as the Hyr'rok'kin commanders directed the foot soldiers her way.

Her men fought to get to her side, but they were walled off by a mob of the panting, drooling monstrosities. The coppery smell of blood was in her nose as Nerthus reconciled herself to her fate, determined to take as many of the foul creatures with her as possible.

But that fate was not to be as a spinning circle of death broke through the wall. Raine was covered in blood, little of it hers, and struck with the force and speed of the gods themselves. Nothing stood before her sword, and anything that dared try was destroyed. Every part of her body was a weapon as she kicked, punched, elbowed, kneed, thrust a sword, parried a thrust, impaled, then head-butted her enemy. She leaped, dived, rolled, turned, jumped, slid, hopped, ducked, and the dozens of Hyr'rok'kin that tried to engage her at any given time could not land a blow. She quickly cleared an area around the Knight Commander and reunited Nerthus with her men before she danced off to another part of battle. The imperials were stunned, never having seen anything like it.

The Hyr'rok'kin were not known to value the lives of their comrades, and the foot soldiers themselves were considered expendable. Knowing this, Raine was prepared when the Hyr'rok'kin archers fired a hail of arrows into the mêlée, a hail that would surely kill more of their own soldiers than the enemy. The thinking was simple and brutal: if they lost a hundred soldiers for every one of the enemy, the smaller force would still be depleted.

But Raine had primed for such a contingency, and the First Scholar of the Ha'kan stood above on the platform and raised her arms. Gimle was not good at destruction magic like Idonea, nor natural magic like Elyara, and she certainly didn't have Skye's extraordinary gifts. But she was very good at one thing: protecting her people. The air above the battling troops shimmered, then solidified into an aqueous form. The arrows bounced harmlessly off the ward. It was the largest shield Gimle had ever conjured, and she couldn't hold it for long. But she didn't need to as the Hyr'rok'kin archers stood stupefied, unable to understand why their arrows weren't working.

Raine smiled and her expression alone was enough to terrify the Hyr'rok'kin around her. But for every one that fled, a dozen more replaced it. She glanced to the imperials, then the Ha'kan. They fought valiantly, but they were starting to get tired, that was evident. And although the Tavinter scouts darted through the fallen Hyr'rok'kin, retrieving arrows, their supply would not last forever. It was time. She gave the signal.

Two dragons swept down over the battlefield, and once past the front line of their own troops, rained down fire on the never-ending supply of Hyr'rok'kin that funneled in. The flow of battle changed in an instant. The Hyr'rok'kin were no longer pressing forward unabated. The winged creatures that had bedeviled those on the grounds now had to deal with an overpowering foe. Talan spun in mid-air and let loose a circle of fire around her, something she had been unable to do with the rope draining her. The flying Hyr'rok'kin screamed in pain and went hurtling into the ground, lighting their own troops on fire. The black dragon dove and dipped, striking out with both claw and fire. The Hyr'rok'kin milled about in terror, running into each another. There was only one escape from the canyon and there were still foot soldiers pouring in, so they crushed one another in their panic.

"Fall back," Raine ordered. It would be best to let the stupid creatures pile in while Talan and Drakar destroyed them. The Ha'kan and imperials began an orderly, coordinated retreat, shields still forward.

And then disaster struck. Raine saw it out of the corner of her eye, what she had feared and what had caused her to delay the attack of the dragons for so long. It was a third catapult, slowly being wheeled through the entrance of the canyon. Talan saw it but it was clear that Drakar did not as he continued to dive low and strafe the Hyr'rok'kin. Raine watched in horror as the great machine was brought to bear and Drakar hovered above the ground.

"Drakar!"

The black dragon turned at the warning roar from his mother, but it was too late. The catapult fired, the golden rope snaked out, and the barbs on its tip hooked into the flesh of Drakar's wing near the webbing where it joined the body. As they had with Talan, the flying Hyr'rok'kin dove in to capture the free end of the rope and wrapped it around any part of the dragon they could. But where they had managed only an ankle with the Ancient Dragon, they got Drakar around the neck. The black dragon plummeted to the earth like a meteor, crushing the Hyr'rok'kin beneath him.

Talan roared in fury as Hell Hounds set upon her son. She dove in, then pulled up short. They were already reloading the catapult, and if they were lucky enough to get her a second time, this battle was over. She wheeled about and swept away in anguish. This one would be up to her love.

And Raine was already calculating the way, her fury fanned by the cries of pain of the fallen dragon and the taunts and shrieks of joy of the Hyr'rok'kin. Drakar had fallen about a fourth of the way into the Hyr'rok'kin army, so a large part of their force was between them. She would not risk the imperials or the Ha'kan to such numbers. She turned and signed an emphatic command to Skye.

Skye drew back. She was not certain she could cast the spell again. But one look at the thrashing, helpless dragon infuriated her. Raine had been specific. Not as large, but it had to be fast. She stood up from her crouched position, raised her hands, generated a ball of light perhaps a third of the size of the previous, then hurled it with all her might directly at Drakar. It was moving fast, much faster than the previous one, and it incinerated a path through the Hyr'rok'kin with demoralizing ease.

And Raine was right behind it, sprinting as fast as she could. Her legs churned, her arms pumped, her lungs burned, and she ran so fast that even the swift Tavinter were stunned. She followed the burning path of destruction the sphere cut through the Hyr'rok'kin, knocking down those few who had the presence of mind to try and stop her. The floating ball cleared the ground troops and burned through a trio of Hell Hounds that weren't smart enough to comprehend the danger. The rest of the beasts realized the peril and backed off from the orb that was floating right towards the dragon. Raine cleared the edge of the mob and with a final burst of speed, launched herself forward and into the ball of light just as it was touching Drakar's skin...

And the ball of light disappeared.

Very slowly, Raine got to her feet. She turned and faced the pack of Hell Hounds and the Hyr'rok'kin army. She drew her short swords, the blue and gold markings standing in bold relief on her forearms and biceps. Her eyes were ice blue as she stood ready to defend the black dragon with her life. The Hyr'rok'kin milled about uncertainly. This was the most dangerous creature in the mortal realm, this they understood. This one had just dismissed, with a touch, the ball of light that had destroyed everything in its path. This one had killed more of their kind than any had in generations, and it had been her people, along with the dragons, that had destroyed their army centuries ago.

But right now, she was outnumbered thousands to one. Her reinforcements were trapped on the other side of an army. Her mages were far away, their power diminished by the distance. That red dragon could not come to her aid without risking capture. And she would risk her own safety to protect the creature lying behind her.

Raine did not care. She twirled her swords about her wrists in a practiced manner. She took a stance, took a deep breath, then spoke in Scinterian the words that her father spoke when facing a hopeless battle.

"Let's play."

The horde screamed and charged.

The sand in front of Raine erupted and the largest wolf that anyone had ever seen exploded from the depths of the earth. He was followed by a pack of wolves that poured forth in an endless stream, black, gray, white, mottled, wolves from the forest, from the plains, from the mountains, from the glacial north, barrel-chested beasts with sharp fangs and glowing eyes. They snarled and charged outward in every direction, meeting the Hell Hounds head on. The gigantic wolf stood upon his hind legs and battled the foot soldiers and Raine joined him at his back. They fought ferociously, losing some of their number, but taking down hundreds for every one that fell. The Hyr'rok'kin were at a loss as to what to do, so did the only thing that they knew. They died one after the other, hoping to wear down their foe.

"We can't keep this up forever," the huge wolf growled.

"I know," Raine said, "let me get Drakar loose, and then we can flee."

She sheathed her swords and ran up onto the back of the fallen dragon. She struggled with the heavy rope, using all her strength to pull the cord from him. But at last she was able to free his neck, and no sooner did the rope touch the ground than the black dragon was on his feet, spewing fire at those behind him.

"Just run!" Raine said, "Before they get the catapult re-aimed!"

Drakar saw the danger as the turret of the weapon was being cranked in his direction. He took two uneven steps, still suffering the effects of the golden rope, and crashed sideways into a crowd of Hyr'rok'kin, crushing them all.

"Well that was effective," he muttered. "Humiliating, but effective." He regained his balance, took two much better steps, and leaped skyward. He was going to wheel about to get Raine, but she shook her head and waved him on.

"What will you do now?" the great wolf asked, shaking then snapping a Hyr'rok'kin in two with his immense jaws.

"We need only to get back to our people," Raine said, "and we can finish this."

Raine leaped upon his back and with a roar, he called his children to him. They stampeded through the throng of Hyr'rok'kin, cleared them, then easily outdistanced them in an all-out retreat. The Hyr'rok'kin screamed as one in rage and frustration. They had brought down a dragon. They had cornered their most coveted prey. And still, this puny gathering of mortals was thwarting them. They regrouped and began marching forward, still vastly outnumbering their enemy despite their losses.

Once at the front lines, Raine leaped from the wolf's back and ran back to the platform upon which Idonea, Elyara, and Gimle were standing. It was clear that Elyara was weakening because Gimle was now supporting her.

"Can you do this?"

Idonea nodded. "I can."

"Good, I'll prepare the counter charge."

Raine gave the order, and the Ha'kan and imperials readied to march forward once more. The Tavinter stood behind them. Raine and the wolves stood at the front.

"And what have you got up your sleeve this time, Scinterian?" Fenrir asked.

Raine grinned. "I believe I have the most powerful mage in Arianthem."

Idonea stood on the raised dais and gazed out at the approaching horde. She was the daughter of a dragon and the protégé of the greatest wizard the world had ever known. The dark magic in her blood stirred, and her mother circled above, feeling the dark magic in her own blood stir in response.

"You can drop the wall," she said calmly.

Elyara collapsed, as did the wall. The Hyr'rok'kin paused in their death march, uncertain what this could mean. They were now free to spread out and attempt to surround the enemy, as had been their original intent. They shouted with rapacious glee and began running forward.

"There are still a lot of them," Nerthus muttered, dismayed to see the number that still remained outside the walls. She felt something hot under her armor, something that went from unpleasant to painful in a fraction of a second. She pulled the chain out from her breastplate, the necklace she wore with the tiny vial of red liquid on it. She dropped it so that the vial rested against the steel of her armor, shaking her hand from the burn.

Raine was also assessing their numbers, but she was more interested to see if there were any more of the catapults remaining. It seemed there was only the one. Also, as the Hyr'rok'kin had again spread out, the depth of their ranks had thinned. She nodded to Idonea.

There were inert piles of sand where the walls had been. These dunes began to shake, tremble, slither about, and then began to flow back towards the small army, almost as if the sand were water. The illusion of liquid was pronounced as it ebbed, surged, then formed a stream that rolled back toward Raine. It began to pool, and the pool became a lake, and then the lake began to swell until it rose up into a single wave. Raine thought the wave would be waist high, perhaps a little more, but it continued to grow. It topped her head, then the head of the great wolf behind her, then it was taller than the Marrow Shards, and still it continued to grow. And as it grew upward, it also grew outward, spreading the entire length of the Hyr'rok'kin army, seeming to take up the extent of the horizon. The size of it was jaw-dropping.

"Well, this is unexpected," Raine said.

And then the gigantic upsurge began to move. It flowed just like a wave across the desert, churning the earth before it like the froth of the sea. It was steep, the distance between the trough and crest the distance between earth and sky. It curled downward, creating a barrel-like effect, as if it were continually on the verge of breaking.

The Hyr'rok'kin, stopped, stunned, then turned and began to run. But it was to no avail as the rapidly growing wave overtook them and swallowed everything in its path. Some were buried, suffocating beneath the heavy sand, some were trapped, unable to move the limbs crushed beneath the surface, some were knocked unconscious and lay scattered like dolls in the wake of the great wave.

"And now we finish this," Raine said, and all followed her charge.

The small army was merciless as it came upon its stunned and helpless foe. Hyr'rok'kin were stabbed, beaten, decapitated, incinerated, crushed, impaled, killed in every way imaginable as the Ha'kan and imperials moved efficiently over their fallen adversaries. The dragons were ruthless, having suffered at their hands, and they burned everything in their path. The catapult, now on its side, was turned to ash. The Tavinter rained down arrows, then ran through the sea of Hyr'rok'kin, stabbing and slicing as they went. Raine was in the lead with the wolves, dealing with those so foolish to stagger to their feet once the wave had passed. It was a bloodbath, but not in the way that anyone would have expected, given the way the day had begun.

Raine slowed, and Fenrir was at her side.

"Are you going to chase them all the way back to the Underworld?" he asked drily.

Raine sighed and sheathed her swords. "No, as much as I want to, that's probably not a good idea."

"And probably not necessary," Fenrir said. The fleeing Hyr'rok'kin numbered in the hundreds, not the tens of thousands that had marched across the Empty Land. The wolf god and the Scinterian, surrounded by wolves, started walking back toward the small army in a comfortable silence.

Queen Halla withdrew her sword from a Hyr'rok'kin foot soldier and paused to look around her. Everything was dead. She looked to her First General, who was dirty, sweaty, and covered in blood, and who had never looked more beautiful to her. And Senta looked upon her Queen, bruised and battered, her armor covered with scrapes, nicks, and cuts, and thought that she had never loved her more. And the Ha'kan as a whole looked to each other, stunned and overjoyed, not only that they had survived, but that they had triumphed.

Nerthus walked through her men, quietly congratulating them, and they felt the same subdued, slightly hysterical elation as the Ha'kan. She came up behind Idonea, just in time to catch her as the raven-haired mage's knees buckled.

"Are you all right?" she asked with concern.

"Of course, I'm all right," Idonea said carelessly, "just a little tired." She noticed the vial outside of Nerthus' armor and grinned wickedly. "Did you really think that little thing could ever control me?"

"Not for an instant," Nerthus replied.

Skye ran to catch up with the Queen and Senta, wanting to make certain they were unharmed. Before she could get a word out, Senta snatched her up and fairly threw her into the air, catching her on the way down and hugging her tightly. She kissed her on the forehead.

"Thank you," she said simply. Senta knew the Tavinter had been the Queen's guardian angel during the fight.

And the Queen knew it as well. "Thank you, First Ranger." Halla grasped Skye's shirt and pulled her to her, treating her as she did all her staff, which was to say she kissed her fully on the mouth, a passionate and prolonged kiss. She released her and moved on to find Astrid, leaving Senta to catch the stunned youngster.

"Welcome to the Royal Staff," Senta said over her shoulder as she followed the Queen.

Raine stood off alone with Fenrir.

"Thank you again, my friend," Raine said, holding the great head in her hands. "I know you will pay for this."

"It's you who I fear will pay," Fenrir said. "My sister will not be happy about this."

"If it comes to that," Raine began, "if—" She trailed off, unable to go on. "Just don't interfere," Raine said, and Fenrir nodded his understanding. The great wolf joined his pack, and the wolves trotted as one back towards the Deep Woods.

Two dragons landed on the expanse of sand, and with a flash of red and yellow light, a silver-haired woman and a devilishly handsome dark-haired man appeared. Idonea had recovered her strength and ran to them, hugging them both tightly. Raine approached, her eyes caressing Talan, then settling on Idonea.

"You...."

"I—," Idonea tried to explain. "I didn't know I was capable of that."

"Yes," Raine said sardonically, "but in the future we might want to lead with that instead of saving it for last." She relented and hugged the raven-haired mage. "That was magnificent."

"I'm very proud of you," Talan agreed, "and I've never been happier that you were born human and not a dragon."

"Hey now," Drakar said, pretending hurt, and Talan kissed him on the forehead. "I'm very proud of you, too, dear."

Drakar was instantly appeased. "And I owe you my life," he said to Raine, growing serious. "You risked all to come save me."

Raine took Talan's hand. "Skye helped, she paved my way. Then Fenrir came to save me."

"I'm not sure he so much as saved you as expedited the process. I'm pretty sure you would have killed everything around you," Drakar said, "it just would have taken all day."

Talan's attention had turned to Raine and she examined the Scinterian with intense focus: bruised and battered, muscles bulging, covered in the blood of her enemies, her eyes a perfect shade of violet.

"You're going to go rape her somewhere, aren't you?" Idonea said.

"Of course, I am," the dragon replied.

CHAPTER 11

The wood elves met the entourage at the edge of the Deep Woods. Word had spread of the epic battle taking place on the plains of the Empty Land, and they were dismayed they were not in time to assist. But they were glad to tend the wounded. Despite the pitched battle, the Ha'kan Queen sent word to her daughter that they would continue their journey. They still had time to reach Mount Alfheim prior to the Ceremony of Assumption. It was decided that the wounded Ha'kan would stay with the wood elves until they were fit to travel. Although the imperials could have returned to their garrisons for treatment, a curious camaraderie had grown between them and their Ha'kan sisters, and they did not wish to leave them, so they, too, remained with the wood elves.

So, after a day's rest, the entourage started out once more. Raine rejoined them and it was a content group that left the Deep Woods, not as lightly celebratory as before, but with a deeper sense of satisfaction, one that came with a hard-fought victory. They had lost few, and those were mourned deeply. But they had beaten an army of monstrosities against impossible odds. Dagna was already hard at work immortalizing the deed, entertaining the troops around her by tossing out lines of the poem she was writing in her head.

Word continued to spread, and the Alfar contingency that was to meet them at the border did not stop there but rode into imperial lands to join them. Raine pulled up as the impressive group of elves, all wearing green and yellow armor, barreled down upon them. They were led by a handsome, fair-haired elf and surprisingly, a dwarf.

Raine dismounted in tandem with the lead elf. He approached Raine, gave her the traditional formal greeting of his people, then embraced her. He put his hands on her shoulders and held her at arm's length.

"You don't appear any worse for the wear," Feyden said.

"Did you expect anything else?"

"Of course not."

The dwarf approached and his greeting was far less restrained. He struck Raine a blow on her shoulder that should have broken her collarbone.

"How could you?" he said. "How could you go into battle without me?"

"I apologize for such egregious conduct," Raine said. "It will never happen again."

"It had better not, lass." And then Lorifal could contain himself no longer and hugged Raine so tightly the Ha'kan winced. "And you two," he said, turning to Elyara and Idonea. "A canyon and a wave of sand? Are the stories true?"

"They are," Dagna said proudly, "and I'm recording them all."

"By my ancestors," Lorifal said, "Dagna, too. If only I could have been there!"

"Feyden," Raine said, "you remember Queen Halla?"

Feyden bowed low. "Of course, your Majesty. I was going to welcome you to the land of the Alfar, but we're not quite there yet."

"Thank you, Feyden. It's good to see you again."

"And the empire has sent us an escort as well, you remember the Knight Commander?"

"Yes," Feyden said smoothly, wondering if he would be chastised for crossing over into imperial territory. Nerthus did no such thing.

"Bristol sends his regards and his congratulations to your sister. He wanted to come, but his words were 'someone has to stay and run the country.'"

Feyden bowed at the unexpected diplomacy from the Knight Commander. Idonea continued to work her magic on that one.

"Shall we get going?" Raine said, putting her arms around the shoulders of the dwarf and elf. "We're cutting our arrival much closer than we intended."

The capital city of the Alfar Republic was extraordinary. Where imperial architecture was designed to project power, size, and force, and Ha'kan to project strength, elegance and beauty, the Alfar were unique in projecting a sense of both history and innovation. The infrastructure was ancient but timeless, meticulously maintained, full of gorgeous detail. The entourage moved slowly through the streets, enthralled with the golden spires that rose into the sky, the intricately carved stone structures that sat perched on the steep cliffs, the towers and walkways that crisscrossed the city. It was a sight that very few non-Alfar had ever seen.

And many of the Alfar came out to greet the visitors. Some were curious about the Ha'kan, and the procession of fearsome, beautiful women did not disappoint. Some wanted to see the Tavinter Rangers, because Alfar scholars speculated that the nomadic people had elven blood somewhere in their bloodline. Although this speculation had been greeted with contempt by many, now, on further review, it seemed possible and even desirable that the Alfar could claim some kinship with these woodland warriors. And the imperials, largely despised by the Alfar, were welcomed because these outmatched soldiers had just fought and destroyed the Hyr'rok'kin in a heroic battle. The Baroness of Fireside garnered particular attention because all wanted to see the raven-haired mage who was rumored to have drowned an army with a wave of sand. And Elyara of the Halvor was greeted with more respect than the Alfar had ever bestowed on any wood elf.

The throngs of elves were slightly disappointed, however, because Ta-lan'alaith'illaria, Queen of all Dragons, and her lover, the Scinterian-Arlan-ian warrior were not present. Out of the illustrious guests, these two went beyond celebrated: they were legends. The soon-to-be Directorate, Maeva, owed some of her political pull to her claimed ties with them, and it was believed that her brother was good friends with the Scinterian. But they were nowhere to be seen, so the crowds had to content themselves with the current spectacle.

The structure housing the High Council was a castle, although with distinctly elven architecture. The gleaming gold turrets grew out of the mountainside, and the structure itself gave the impression of solidity while perched precariously on the sheer cliffs. The procession stopped at the bottom of an immense staircase. Queen Halla dismounted and began to flow gracefully up the stairs, her staff one step behind. To the wonder of those standing on the upper terrace, the soon-to-be Directorate started to flow down the stairs toward her. The Emperor had received no such honor; Maeva had made him climb the entire staircase. But she clearly considered the Ha'kan more favorably, for she met the Queen on the middle terrace, a point of etiquette not lost on her people.

"Your Majesty," Maeva said, bowing low to the Ha'kan Queen.

"Madame Directorate," Halla said, giving the deep curtsy of one sovereign to another. Maeva was greatly pleased with the grace and respect of the Ha'kan. Civility, tradition, and ceremony ruled the Alfar, and the

Ha'kan appeared kindred souls on these matters. She nodded a greeting to her brother, then addressed the Queen again.

"I understand you had a little skirmish on the way here," Maeva said, her tone signifying she knew the skirmish had been anything but.

"A bit of a diversion," the Queen said, and Maeva appreciated the tact and steel of the response.

Maeva extended her arm to Halla. "I must hear every detail," she said. "But let us finish our ascent to I can greet the rest of your entourage properly."

And then the throngs received a rare treat, for the cold, arrogant aristocrat walked up the staircase arm-in-arm with the gorgeous Queen of the Ha'kan, when on most occasions she would not deign to touch another. At the top of the staircase, Melwen, Maeva's Chief Assistant, bowed low as his liege passed. The First General, taller than all present, nodded in recognition as she moved by him. A minor council member leaned in to whisper to him.

"I didn't imagine the Ha'kan were so large."

"I told you they were big," Melwen whispered back.

They entered into a grand foyer, and there were throngs of spectators here, as well. Maeva now turned to the Ha'kan Royal Staff.

"High Priestess, welcome to Mount Alfheim. I'm certain you'll be inundated with ill-mannered questions, so please let me know if anyone becomes too boorish."

"Alfar courtesy is well-known," Astrid said, "and I'm used to curious questions about my people."

Maeva moved to Gimle. "First Scholar, you already have many claims on your time. My scholars wish to discuss history with you, Kiren wants to talk linguistics, and your skill with wards has now drawn the attention of my mages. Don't let them exhaust you."

"It will be my pleasure to discuss all these things. I look forward to it."

Maeva moved to Senta, then just stood in front of her looking her up and down. "And First General, please don't intimidate my soldiers too much."

Senta grinned. "I think there's little danger in that. I saw the Alfar on display in Haldis. Your military excellence is well-known, Madame Directorate."

Maeva turned to Skye, who was standing slightly behind the First General.

"And this is now your First Ranger," Maeva said, and Senta took note that the Alfar spy network was as proficient as always.

Skye bowed in the Tavinter custom, showing far more poise than Maeva had seen from the girl in the past, although a blush colored her cheeks and made her lovelier than ever.

"Madame Directorate."

Maeva would be kind for once and not toy with her, although there would be time enough for that, later. She moved on to the ravishing woman next to her whose plunging bodice captured the attention of even the most reserved of the Alfar.

"Ah, Baroness," Maeva said sardonically. The title was something of a joke between them. Maeva knew that Raine had bestowed it upon Idonea simply to get out of a tedious imperial function. Upon Idonea's dramatic entrance, Maeva had been the first to buy in on the ruse, solidifying Idonea's place in the imperial court. The mage's laughing dark eyes communicated the inside joke.

"Madame Directorate, it's a pleasure to see you again. May I present my brother, Drakar."

Maeva turned to the rakishly handsome young man, pleased with this unexpected guest. Dark hair, dark eyes, a faint physical resemblance to his sister and a very strong non-physical one. They shared the same sexual energy, full of magic and irreverence, and an impudence that was irresistible.

"Ah yes, the black dragon I saw in the Ha'kan capital. Are you going to rape and pillage your way through Alfar society?"

Drakar bowed exaggeratedly low in self-mocking. "Not without your permission, Madame Directorate."

Idonea slapped him on the arm, and Maeva noted the same, intriguing sexual tension between the two. The gossips in court were going to have a field day. "And you remember the Knight Commander Nerthus?" Idonea continued.

"Yes," Maeva said, pulling the identity from the endless catalogue her network provided. Apparently Idonea led this one around on a leash. "Welcome to Mount Alfheim, Knight Commander. I understand your troops fought bravely."

"Thank you, Madame Directorate," Nerthus said, lacking the charm of all those before her, but responding with a frank honesty that slightly elevated her in Maeva's eyes. What elevated Nerthus the most, however, was that the Knight Commander routinely bedded the hellcat standing next to her, a deed provoking inestimable admiration.

"And the Imperial Bard," Maeva said to Dagna, "present in yet another epic adventure. Will you immortalize this one as well?"

"I have already begun, Madame Directorate," Dagna said proudly.

"Excellent, we look forward to its completion. And Elyara," Maeva said, greeting the slender wood elf by name. "Thank you for coming. I regret that Y'arren could not attend, but I understand."

"Thank you, Madame Directorate. Y'arren has sent a blessing to be bestowed upon you during your Ceremony."

"I am honored to accept such a gift," Maeva said. "And we welcome you not simply as Y'arren's substitute, but in your own right as well. I understand you played a pivotal role in this latest victory. And I think Kiren has anticipated your arrival more than any other, with the possible exception of Raine."

"Speaking of which," Maeva said, glancing about, "where is Raine? And your mother?" She said to Idonea.

"They didn't wish to pull attention away from the matter-at-hand," Idonea said, "Although they've promised to be here for the Reception and Ceremony."

Maeva leaned close. "They're off fucking somewhere, aren't they?"

"No doubt," Idonea said.

"Of course they are," Drakar agreed.

CHAPTER 12

Mount Alfheim was already in a state of celebration, and with the arrival of the newcomers, the merriment only increased. The Ha'kan attracted non-stop attention, and there was a mutual fascination between the High Elves and the all-female race. Several elven women in the nobility sought to try their hand with the Royal Guard and found the Ha'kan surprisingly willing, not having completely grasped that sex was yet another form of diplomacy for the Ha'kan. The First General had cautioned the Guard on the differences between their cultures, but then told them to use their best judgment and discretion. They did so with remarkable success, furthering the goodwill between their peoples and giving the elven women a night they would carry to their grave.

Queen Halla met with the Emperor, who thanked her for defending imperial territory against the Hyr'rok'kin assault. The imperials who had accompanied the Emperor were in awe of their comrades who had fought in the Empty Land. They expressed disappointment that they had missed the fight. The fidelity of the veterans of that battle toward the Ha'kan impressed itself upon the soldiers not present in the battle, and soon they were all drinking and telling tales together. The contingency of dwarves that accompanied Lorifal were also deeply depressed they had missed the battle and joined in with the Ha'kan for both the drinking and the storytelling.

The Tavinter and the Alfar got along remarkably well, strange for two such disparate races. It was further proof in the minds of the elven scholars that the Tavinter were indeed an offshoot of the ancient elves, for they were a striking and well-formed people, shy in demeanor, charmingly self-effacing, but deadly in stealth. The Rangers constantly startled those around them, and Skye ordered her people to make more noise, so they did not sneak up on everyone.

Kiren, the young companion of the future Directorate, was overjoyed at the presence of Gimle and Elyara. She had a decidedly scholarly bent that had impressed the Alfar, even those who had at first been predisposed to dislike her. When rumor floated back that Maeva had taken an imperial human as a lover, it sparked outrage. An entire contingent of the High Elven Council was prepared to censure Maeva upon her return from the imperial land. That drive for censure dissolved upon first sight of the girl. She was gentle, brilliant, humble, and stunningly beautiful, with dark blue eyes and a languorous dreamy air that sparked a strange, quixotic lust in almost everyone around her. She was fluent in multiple languages, a skilled artist and musician, and had a grasp and knowledge of history that was astonishing. In short, she was everything that humans were not, or at least not what the elves perceived them to be. The elven scholars immediately claimed her as their own, and what should have been a devastating political faux pas for Maeva instead added to her cachet.

The day of the Reception arrived, and a great throng filled the grand hall. Alfar, Ha'kan, Imperial, Dwarf, and Tavinter all mixed freely wearing their finest garments. The Alfar were a picture of stately grace. The Ha'kan were sensual, regal, and elegant. The imperials were stylish and well-tailored. The armor of the dwarves was lavish and ornate. The clothing of the Tavinter was simple but striking.

In fact, the Tavinter clothing was so soft it compelled the touch. Prior to the alliance with the Ha'kan, Tavinter casual wear had been utilitarian: the skins of animals they had killed when hunting. The Ha'kan took those clothes and made them into something harshly beautiful, the tanned leather giving way to the suede of the underside of the skin. The resulting clothes were slightly less durable, but so soft they obliged one to touch them. Skye was subject to this compulsion by many at the fête and made the mistake of commenting on it to Senta. Senta replied that yes, her clothing must be the only reason why everyone was fondling her. Gimle hid a smile at the dry comment.

The Queen was even lovelier than usual, and she and Astrid were surrounded by a group of elven nobility. Idonea was making the rounds with her brother, and true to Maeva's prediction, the two generated scandalous speculation as to their relationship as they moved about arm-in-arm. Both Nerthus and Dagna had been drawn into duty by the Emperor, who was having little luck with interaction beyond strained conversation. But once he was joined by his Knight Commander and his Official Bard, both survivors of the recent mêlée, his company became more desirable. The two women were able to entertain his guests with descriptions of the epic battle.

Elyara was in a group of elven mages and scholars engaged in intense discussion, and many were surprised that Kiren was in this group, for rarely was the girl allowed out of Maeva's reach. Although Maeva's gaze would occasionally settle on her prize, she trusted Elyara, if for no other reason than the wood elf was so in love with that silly bard of hers that infidelity was out of the question. Feyden made the rounds in the service of his sister, but on this day, it was far less painful than normal. He genuinely enjoyed the company of the Tavinter and the Ha'kan, probably even more so than his own people. And Lorifal immediately inserted himself in the midst of the Royal Guard, because no one could drink like those Ha'kan warriors.

Skye saw a couple she knew and pushed her way through the crowd. The first was a woman in a blue-green gown that set off a pair of stunning, aquamarine eyes. Her companion was a roguishly good-looking woman wearing finery with the grace of a stage actor rather than an actual noble. The first looked to Skye with pleasure and the second with obvious relief.

"Jorden, Syn!" Skye exclaimed, and ran to them. She hugged both women.

"I was hoping you would be here," Syn said.

"You're not here on business, are you?" Skye said.

It was a valid concern, for few people in the room knew that the Lady Jorden was actually Lagmann, the head of the Guild of Thieves, and that Syn was the best thief in all of Arianthem.

"No, no," Jorden replied, "Maeva is a very old friend of mine."

"Oh," Skye said, relieved. "That's right."

"Why don't you go take my love over to the bar," Jorden suggested, "and I will go mix as I should."

Syn was enormously grateful to be excused. She had no issue with her lover moving about in high society. The Lady Jorden was an imperial noblewoman and subject to that expectation. Syn, on the other hand, was a rogue and a thief, and her only expectation was to park herself in front of a beer. That, and to try and resist the temptation to fleece some of these people.

They moved to the side of the hall, and Syn poured herself a beer and Skye a cider. Skye had become one of her best friends through common adventures, and one of the few who had never looked down upon her due to her station. Skye was so unassuming that Syn had no idea she was the Tavinter ruler until months after meeting her.

"I wanted to thank you again for coming for me," Skye said, "when I was captive in the Deep Woods."

"You would have done it for me," Syn said.

"You're right," Skye said. She caught sight of the Emperor and giggled into her cup. "Didn't you sneak into his bedroom and steal his scepter?"

"That I did," Syn said. "Even wrote my name on his forehead, and he slept through the whole thing."

For whatever reason, the reminder of this escapade made Syn feel a little bit better about herself. She glanced to the woman who would become Directorate in the Ceremony of Assumption tomorrow, and then felt even better. That theft had helped put Maeva on her throne, or whatever the elven equivalent of it was. Life was certainly strange, Syn mused, all of the events that led her to break into a cottage in the wilderness, meet Raine, fall in love with the Lady Jorden, meet Skye, and now be invited to the supreme social event in all of Arianthem.

"Aeric is here," Skye said, "he's going to want to see you."

"Oh, good," Syn said, even more relieved. She had been adopted by the Tavinter, accepted as one of their own. She dearly loved the forest people, even though she was terrified of the forest. And she really liked that dwarf, Lorifal, who loved to drink as much as she did.

All was going well, drink was flowing, the food was spectacular, the conversation was witty and urbane. Ancient rivals were finding common ground. New friendships were forming. Assignations were being discreetly planned for the coming evening. The Alfar would soon have a new leader of their High Council, and this was a cause for celebration. Nothing could distract these guests from having a good time.

Nothing except a great thud that shook the castle walls. Conversation stopped and many looked about fearfully. The Ha'kan, however, were remarkably composed, for they had felt this many times and merely smiled. Maeva herself looked only pleased.

"I believe my guests of honor have arrived," she murmured, then excused herself from the group around her. She moved to the bottom of the staircase that led up to the private terrace, then waited there expectantly. This was strange to many, because the terrace had no access from the outside and the drop was straight down the face of a cliff. There was a collective gasp as brilliant flash of yellow light appeared through the windows, illuminating the dusk sky.

Then two figures appeared at the top of the stairs, and all understood.

The first was a dazzling silver-haired woman, tall, lean, with glowing amber eyes set in noble, patrician features. She wore red armor that danced with flame and curved about her body as if it were part of her. This armor was more regal, more ceremonial than that which she normally wore, with not quite as many spikes. She also wore a full, flowing, white-and-gold cape that accentuated her supremacy, and a gold circlet on her head that, although simple in design, declared her royalty more emphatically than the most vulgar of crowns. Power emanated from her as she exuded a dark sensuality that snaked out and wrapped itself around every person in the room. The Ha'kan luxuriated in the sensation.

And on her arm was an individual, completely different, yet no less extraordinary. The young woman was stunningly beautiful: striking chiseled features, flaxen hair, and startling blue eyes. She was lithely muscular, serenely confident, and wore the gorgeous raiment of a tragic, lost race. She projected power of a different sort, a raw physicality that would subdue one through sheer brute force if necessary. But as she turned to her companion, it was as if she became another person. Her features softened, her eyes turned violet, and there was a youthful and angelic beauty about her as she looked on one whom she so obviously adored. That change in appearance produced desire in the assembly as a whole, everything from gentle longing to uncontrolled lust.

As these two other-worldly creatures started down the stairs to the assembly below, Maeva had a remarkable and humbling insight. True, she was about to be appointed the head of the Alfar Republic. The powerful Queen of the Ha'kan was here, the ruler of the Tavinter was present, members of the Dwarven High Council were in attendance, and the Emperor himself was in the audience.

But these two, they were the true royal couple. Without a land or people, these two were the undisputed rulers of Arianthem itself. The Queen of all Dragons and the Scinterian-Arlanian were creatures of myth, living, breathing legends, defenders and protectors of all beneath them. Free to do as they would, they sacrificed time and again to save others. And the assembly as a whole seemed to become aware of this same epiphany, viewing their arrival with near reverence.

"She certainly knows how to make an entrance, doesn't she?" Drakar murmured into his sister's ear.

"That she does," Idonea murmured back.

When the couple reached the bottom of the steps, Maeva bowed deeply, displaying more respect to this pair than she had ever displayed to anyone. Talan bowed slightly, her air enigmatic and distant as always. But to Raine, the weight of ceremony was becoming oppressive. She took Maeva's hand in her own and bent to brush a chivalrous kiss across it. Her manner was playful, mischievous, even a trace flirtatious, and it immediately broke the ice. The room let out its collective breath.

"Madame Directorate," Raine said formally, "thank you for inviting us to your Ceremony."

"Thank you for coming," Maeva said, "the honor is all mine."

"What did they do with your sister?" Lorifal whispered to Feyden, "And who is that imposter in her place?" He grunted at Feyden's sharp elbow in his side.

"I understand that Arianthem once again owes you thanks," Maeva said, "for rising to protect our lands."

"This one would never pass up an opportunity to kill Hyr'rok'kin," Talan said, reclaiming the hand she had briefly relinquished.

"Nor you," Raine replied.

"Nor I," Talan agreed.

Lorifal pushed through the crowd, dismissing the awe that kept everyone else back. "It's about time you got here," he said. "I brought you some amber sting, made special by some of my kin."

Raine's eyes glowed at the thought of the wicked drink. Most could not consume it without going blind or collapsing in a heap, but it was Raine's favorite. It was also one of Talan's favorites as it affected Raine by lowering her inhibitions and increasing her libido.

"For my sake," Talan said, "thank you, Lorifal."

Lorifal's stature amongst the Alfar skyrocketed. For him to speak so casually to the exalted pair instantly increased his standing. There was an aloofness to the dragon that did not encourage approach, and only those who personally knew the two dared come close. Feyden was obviously in such lofty company.

"Raine, thank you so much for coming," the fair-haired elf said, then embraced her. This drew numerous raised eyebrows, for Maeva's brother was even more reserved than the Directorate herself. And the fact that the Scinterian warrior warmly returned his embrace satisfied those who doubted the tales of their friendship.

These exchanges became a spectator sport of sort as people ranked the greetings. Anyone who dared approach the dragon and her lover were automatically ranked higher than everyone else at the assembly. Maeva had received extremely high marks because, after all, they had responded to her invitation. Lorifal and Feyden were given points because of their relaxed familiarity with Raine, and because the dragon appeared to tolerate them. The spectators watched with interest as the Ha'kan approached.

Queen Halla gave a deep curtsy and Talan bowed in return.

"Are you enjoying yourself?" Raine asked.

"Most definitely," Halla said, "it's a delightful reception."

"And are your people attracting curiosity?" Talan asked.

Halla deferred to her High Priestess. "Yes," Astrid said, "it's strange to explain our ways to others because it seems so natural to us. I've been repeatedly asked about 'jealousy' and whether or not we feel it for one another. It's difficult to explain that this is rare and considered an illness in our culture."

"I've been asked the same thing," Gimle added. "I explained that the Ha'kan once had their own language, before we adopted the common tongue. There was no word for 'jealousy' in the ancient dialect."

"Hmm," Talan said, "the dragons have eighteen different words for it."

This drew laughter from the group as Talan stood behind Raine and wrapped her arms about her.

"And yet somehow that seems perfectly appropriate," Senta said.

The comfortable conversation and easy laughter of the group gave the Ha'kan very high marks with the spectators. It was clear that the Queen and her staff had a long-standing and mutually respectful relationship with the Scinterian and the dragon. The elven mage, Elyara, also received a warm welcome, especially from Raine, but the dragon displayed a bit of fondness toward the slender wood elf as well.

Humorously, the Emperor was ranked far lower than either his Bard or Knight Commander in this impromptu contest. Both Nerthus and Dagna were greeted with enthusiasm by Raine, while she greeted the Emperor with mere politeness. The dragon greeted the Bard, gave the Knight Commander a knowing stare, and barely acknowledged the Emperor. The Tavinter ruler received extremely high marks because she hugged the Scinterian and the deep camaraderie between the two was evident. The dragon even deigned to tease her, which was evident by the Scinterian's laughter and the Tavinter's blush. The Lady Jorden and her mysterious companion approached, and the onlookers peered around one another to watch the show.

"Jorden," Raine said, extending her arms, and Jorden gave her a peck on each cheek.

"Raine, it's so good to see you again. Talan," Jorden said, more formally.

Talan's amber eyes slid to Syn. "Ah, my little thief."

Syn managed to look even more uncomfortable than she had throughout the evening. Her eyes went to the bracelet around Talan's wrist.

"I see you still have the fade bracelet."

The dragon smiled, which was sometimes worse than her frown.

"I wear it always."

The bystanders noted that the Lady Jorden appeared to have a professional relationship with the Scinterian whereas her companion's seemed to be more personal. And the dragon treated the companion with something close to disdain. But even the disdain garnered points because it bespoke of familiarity and some sort of deeper relationship. The dragon appeared quite entertained by the roguish figure.

One of the more interesting interactions of the evening came about when Maeva's young lover approached the pair, and there was a strange, intense exchange between Kiren and Raine. The young woman embraced the Scinterian for an extended period of time, then Raine placed her hands on the young woman's shoulders and they had a quiet conversation. The dragon was content to stand back while this lengthy conversation took place. There was a gentleness in the Scinterian's manner that she had displayed with no one, and those closest to her could swear that her eyes were violet as she spoke to the girl. Finally, Raine released her and they parted. The Scinterian seemed almost a trace melancholy as the silver-haired woman took her in her arms. And most surprisingly, Maeva had watched the entire exchange without jealousy, merely a thoughtful look on her face.

The dragon had shown little regard or attention throughout the night. It was not that she was rude; she was merely disinterested, as might be expected from a thousand-year-old creature of enormous power. The one exception to this was when the raven-haired mage and her brother approached, and the dragon kissed them both and held them with affection. It was then that the shock of understanding went through the assembly that these were the dragon's children, and an avalanche of implications crushed down upon many, not the least of whom was the Emperor, who could not fathom how he did not know that the Baroness of Fireside was the daughter of a dragon. And the Scinterian appeared to occupy a quasi-parental role, both friend and peer to the youngsters, but clearly respected and loved by them. It was perhaps the most extraordinary family gathering anyone had ever seen.

Finally, Raine and Talan were left alone for a brief period, and they were content to stand back and enjoy one another's company. It was simple to pick out the snippets of conversation throughout the hall since both of their hearing was abnormally acute.

"—did you hear? There were tens of thousands of Hyr'rok'kin—"

"—I have never seen Feyden embrace anyone—"

"—she built a canyon, from the sand, to change the terrain—"

"—do you think that mage sleeps with her brother?"

"—they said the Scinterian fought like one of the gods, killed thousands—"

"—what I wouldn't give for our High Priestess to look like that—"

"—the Tavinter wields some strange light magic, a ball of sorts—"

"—the Queen of the Ha'kan led her troops into battle, can you see the Emperor—"

"—they say she is also Arlanian. I brushed up against her and it was exquisite, such a surge of lust—"

"—they said it was a wave made out of sand, swept away the enemy—"

"—those Tavinter make no noise at all—"

"—how do you think Maeva knows the Lady Jorden?"

"—flying Hyr'rok'kin, can you imagine it? What else—"

"—can you imagine the two of them in bed together?"

This last conversation caused Raine to turn to Talan, for it was about them. "Why does everyone want to imagine us in bed?"

Talan laughed her low, throaty laugh. "Do you have to ask? Dragons are known for their lust. You are both Arlanian and Scinterian, offspring of the greatest lovers and fighters of all time. I enjoy imagining it anytime I'm not actually doing it."

"Do you know," Raine continued, "that the dwarves have a statue of us, you in dragon form and me naked?"

"I would like to see that." She ran her fingers through Raine's hair. "And there have been many incidents. Remember the wood elves at my altar?"

Raine grinned. Yes, there had been many times where the two had been caught in the act, most of the time so engrossed in one another they were unaware until they were finished. And even when they were aware, they didn't stop unless they were in danger. One had to have priorities.

"I'm sure those accounts spread far and wide," Talan said.

The Reception was a great success and the tired throng went to bed happy. Maeva retired with her young lover. The Ha'kan Royal Staff all retired together. The dragon's daughter retired alone, but Maeva's agents reported that the Knight Commander soon joined her in her suite. The dragon's son was reported to be entertaining four women at the same time. Maeva had politely inquired of Talan if she wished to sleep on the Terrace, but the dragon declined, saying she would remain in human form for the night, and retired with Raine to their suite.

Throughout the evening, Skye had carefully avoided the subtle and un-subtle offers she had received, even those from the Royal Guard, and for a very specific reason. She returned to her suite, alone, then stood gazing out her window at the night sky. The stars were dim, washed out in the bright light of the full moon.

Skye did not know it, but Raine, too, stood gazing out at the moon, waiting expectantly. She turned to Talan, who also waited.

"She's here."

Skye turned around at the light that glowed in her room, the radiance of the portal that opened, then enlarged. A woman with white hair, lovely pale skin, fine features, red lips, and divine breasts, stepped through the portal. She was furious.

"And did you forget our bargain so soon?"

"Of course not," Skye said, calmly ignoring the sorceress' anger. "I'm at your disposal."

Ingrid's eyes narrowed. She was enjoying the righteous anger she felt and did not want this whelp to diffuse it.

"You would leave with me now?" Ingrid asked. "If I demand it?"

"Of course. I would never go back on my word. But—," Skye continued on before the sorceress could interject, "I have an alternate proposal."

"What?" Ingrid said, crossing her arms and momentarily distracting Skye with the breasts that pushed upward.

"I—," she shook her head, clearing her senses. "I propose that you stay here with me instead."

"Stay here with you?" Ingrid said, incredulous. "You're just going to stay confined to this room, let me fuck you right through the Ceremony of Assumption?"

"Well," Skye said calmly, "that is one possibility. Or, we could get that out of our systems tonight, and you could attend the ceremony with me tomorrow."

"What?" Ingrid asked, flabbergasted.

"I was invited as the leader of the Tavinter, and my invitation specified that I could bring a guest. You could be my guest."

"You're asking me on a date?" Ingrid said, her incredulity now full-blown disbelief.

"I am."

Ingrid had to sit down. She stared across at the girl who was proving to be a far more wily opponent than she had ever imagined. She tapped her lower lip with her fingertip, trying to fathom this development. Finally, she gave up and accepted she might not ever understand this Tavinter.

"Fine," she said, "but get over here."

Skye got to her feet and obediently approached, the sorceress. "Do you want my blood?"

"Not right now," Ingrid said, surprising Skye. She snatched the girl and threw her face-down, bent over the bed, exciting them both. She skillfully loosened Skye's breeches and dropped them to her knees on the floor, then thrust her fingers up inside of her. The girl was already wet, telling Ingrid that they were equally aroused by the situation. And they had a common goal, for Ingrid was tired of the girl's calm demeanor, and Skye wanted nothing more than to lose control to those skilled fingers. And the sorceress worked a different kind of magic, subjugating the young woman completely until she moaned and thrashed about, giving in to the skill of that hand. And it brought the sorceress enormous pleasure as she dominated the Tavinter leader, thinking the only thing better would be for Tova to hear her offspring cry out the sorceress' name in the throes of unrestrained passion.

Several rooms away, the tension drained from Raine's shoulders and she relaxed. She moved away from the window and joined her lover in bed.

CHAPTER 13

The Ceremony was to begin mid-morning, giving the late night revelers a chance to sleep in. Everyone began gathering once more in the great hall. Raine appeared, again dressed in Arlanian clothing, and this time Talan was not at her side. This was not unusual, for the dragon often slept late, and Raine was happy to handle their social obligations. Although no one would speak of it, many were glad, for the Scinterian was far more approachable alone than she had been with the intimidating presence of the Queen of all Dragons. She moved through the company in a relaxed manner, and all were subject to the longing ache that the charismatic Arlanian produced. When Idonea began hanging off her, the tongues began wagging even more furiously than they had with Drakar.

The Queen was wondering where Skye was, and Senta was just preparing to retrieve her when Skye appeared in the doorway. Her arrival caused many to pause in their conversation. There was a lovely woman on her arm, another creature of dark power, and it was apparent that many in the room knew her, and if not displeased, were at least startled by her presence. The Ha'kan, particularly, gazed at her with expressions of reserve.

"Well isn't this fun," Idonea murmured.

Raine took it upon herself to stride across the hushed room, Idonea in tow. She released Idonea's arm and stepped forward, stopping directly in front of the couple. She examined the sorceress for a moment, then gave her a short bow.

"Ingrid," she said politely.

"Scinterian," the sorceress said, cold but cordial.

Raine examined Skye, who looked unharmed and did not appear to be under duress. "Is this your guest?"

"It is," Skye said firmly.

"Very well," Raine said, then gave another stiff bow to Ingrid. "Welcome to Mount Alfheim, then." Idonea recaptured Raine's arm as the Scinterian spun on her heel.

"Let me know if you want to play," Idonea said over her shoulder, her eyes full of dark mirth, and the two began walking back across the room.

The room let out its collective breath while the sorceress sent a fuming glance at the back of the departing mage. The dragon's daughter was the only mage in Arianthem more powerful than she and had been besting her in their last conflict before she was forced to leave, a fact that Idonea had just reminded her of with the taunt.

"You just couldn't resist, could you?" Raine said under her breath.

"Of course, I couldn't," Idonea said. "When do I ever pass up an opportunity like that?"

"Never."

"Is everything all right?" Senta asked as they approached, her eyes still on the sorceress across the room.

"Yes," Raine said. "Everything is fine. Skye does this of her own free will."

The Ha'kan stared at Skye and the sorceress, wary, but without judgment. It was a legitimate way of dealing with the situation, but that did not make it less dangerous.

"She's always been reckless," Senta said of Skye, "even at the Academy. That's a Tavinter trait."

Maeva had observed the scene, and now Raine excused herself to speak with the Directorate.

"So let me get this straight," Maeva said, "the Tavinter is now fucking her mortal enemy?"

Raine had to smile at the crude, but highly accurate summary. Maeva wielded profanity as skillfully as she did flowery prose.

"Yes, that's about right. It's the Ha'kan way," Raine said.

"So," Maeva mused, "if I went over there and declared war on Queen Halla...?"

Raine burst into laughter. "Trust me, there are far easier ways with the Ha'kan."

The situation seemed to be defused, so everyone returned to their gossip, although they continued to cast curious stares at the sorceress. Skye made her way around the room, providing polite introductions, the most awkward of which was when she introduced Ingrid to Syn, forgetting they had already met on several occasions.

"Ah yes," Ingrid said, "the thief who stole something precious from me."

Syn cleared her throat, clearly uneasy around the sorceress.

"You're in good company, then," Jorden said, "right up there with the Emperor."

Ingrid turned her attention to the noblewoman. There was something intriguing there, an underlying steel that was not evident in her outward gentility. This woman was more than she appeared.

"Indeed," the sorceress said, liking the noblewoman more for whatever dark secret she held. They moved on.

"Whatever do you think Skye is doing?" Jorden asked.

"I saw that woman naked. I know exactly what she's doing," Syn said, earning a slap from Jorden.

The sorceress was coldly polite to everyone with an air of arrogance that trumped even that of the very arrogant Alfar. But no one outdid a dragon. When Talan strode into the room, she passed aloofly through the crowd with stately grace, giving the sorceress a glance that indicated she was of little consequence. Ingrid would have burned at the slight had Talan not treated everyone exactly the same way, all but Raine.

Raine was about to greet her love when she grew very cold and the markings on her back and shoulders surfaced on her skin. She turned to face whatever danger had appeared and was confronted by a pair of pale blue-green eyes staring out from underneath a dark cloak. The woman possessed a funereal beauty and was amused by the response she could elicit from this warrior.

"Hello, Raine."

Raine frowned. "Hello Mal—, Pernilla," she said, correcting herself. She spoke under her breath, because to speak that name aloud doomed all who overheard it. "I trust you're here on pleasure and not business."

"I'm here on business, of course," she said, and Raine braced herself to do battle. "But you must remember, I'm the Emperor's most trusted advisor, and that is the capacity in which I attend this function."

"Oh," Raine said, unclenching her fists, "right."

The vampyre's cold gaze caressed the Scinterian warrior, an ambiguous look with an intent somewhere between rape and cannibalism.

"You paid the price for the safety of the people here. I keep my bargains. But I'll come find you if I get thirsty."

"Hello, Pernilla," Talan said, interjecting herself firmly in the middle of their conversation. Pernilla found the rescue of the fearsome warrior beyond entertaining, and she bestowed on Talan the same look of sensual malevolence she had on Raine.

"Hello, Talan," Pernilla said.

Raine had long ago reconciled herself to running into Talan's ex-lovers, for the list was endless, but the head of the Shadow Guild, the elite of all assassins, was probably the most dangerous. Well, Raine thought, the most dangerous save one.

"Are you harassing my love?" Talan asked.

"Of course, I am. And it's your fault," Pernilla said, "I can't help myself. You gave me her blood, and now I have a taste for it."

Talan turned Raine around by the shoulder and began to lead her away as if she were a child. "I'll remember that," Talan said, looking back, "if I ever need something."

"Thank you," Raine said, uncharacteristically flustered. "That woman gets under my skin."

"That's not surprising," Talan said, "when she took your blood, it was probably the closest you've ever been to a sexual experience outside of our relationship."

"I don't really want to think about that," Raine said darkly. Just then, Raine caught sight of another vampyre, one she was also familiar with. This was Pernilla's second in command, the true Malron'a, and Raine had battled this beauty on several occasions.

"Hello, Raine," the vampyr said in a sultry voice as she passed.

"Have I mentioned how much I hate vampyres?" Raine muttered.

"And have I mentioned how much they like you?" Talan replied.

The vampyr pushed past Feyden and Lorifal and they both did a double-take, then looked at Raine.

"Isn't that—?"

"Yes," Raine said, "but it's of no concern." At their baffled looks, she sighed. "It's a very long story, and I'll explain later. But no one is in any danger."

"No one but Raine," Talan said, laughing as she strolled away.

The Ceremony of Assumption began with all of the pomp and fanfare expected of the Alfar. It was filled with solemn tradition, ancient ritual, and even a few sacraments. The blessing bestowed by Elyara on behalf of Y'arren was given particular prominence. Although the High Elves often looked down upon their Wood Elf brethren, Y'arren was the oldest living of either race and was revered by all.

Maeva was grand and noble, accepting the position of Directorate with the dignity and refinement that her people expected. The Ceremony was the same as it had been since time immemorial, the only deviation being the young human that stood at the Directorate's side, one that, unbeknownst to but a few, had Arlanian blood in her veins from some ancestor generations before.

In short, it went flawlessly. Despite the fact that long-term rivals were present, despite the fact that wildly dissimilar cultures were mixing, despite the fact that both the head of the Thieves Guild and the Assassin's Guild were in attendance, despite all of these potentially explosive factors, the Ceremony went impeccably. It helped that a very small band of Ha'kan, Tavinter, and imperials had fought with the aid of a dragon, her children, and the last Scinterian just days before, and had destroyed a massive invading force of Hyr'rok'kin. For all that could have gone wrong, it was a perfect moment for all of the peoples of Arianthem.

The celebration went long into the night and started up again the next morning almost without pause. The revelers had gotten a few hours' sleep, then rose to begin anew. The dwarves had drunk enough the night before that they were still cheerfully inebriated when they woke. The Royal Guard insisted on a brief training exercise, joined by the Tavinter, and Raine took advantage of the chance to train. The Alfar guards watched the swordplay enviously, and Raine lightheartedly challenged them as well. Soon the elves experienced firsthand what they already knew from observation: the Scinterian was without equal. Their duties done for the day, the Ha'kan and Tavinter rejoined the festivities.

Couches had been brought into the great hall and the atmosphere was relaxed as people lounged about. Maeva moved amongst her own people and her guests, skillfully building all the political connections she would ever need. Nerthus and Dagna were still stuck at the Emperor's side, but now his most-trusted advisor hovered over him, bringing him more comfort than they ever could. Raine found this funny, given the true identity of his 'advisor,' but she tried not to pay too much attention to her because it would bring those pale eyes in her direction where they would settle for an extended period of time. The food was excellent, the delicacies of the elven chefs both exotic and delicious. It was another perfect day.

"And where is your sorceress?" Raine asked.

Skye shrugged. "I told her she could stay despite the bargain, and that just made her angry. She left last night."

Raine shrugged also. "Strange, yet like her."

"I agree." Skye eyed the buffet table. "I'm going to get some food. Do you want anything?"

"No," Raine said, "I'm fine."

Skye started across the room. Then abruptly stopped.

The feeling of loss swept over Raine so suddenly she closed her eyes. Talan tilted her chin up and looked to the southeast. Elyara bowed her head, then put it in her hands. Idonea swallowed hard and blinked to keep the hot tears from falling.

The elven mages were uneasy, looking one to the other, unable to identify the feeling that swept over them but feeling it all the same. Maeva was aware of the disruption, unable to feel it herself but sensing it in the dismay of the others. Whatever it was, it appeared to affect only those closely attuned to magic. The Ha'kan were oblivious, confused at the behavior, except for their First Scholar who had a look of growing understanding on her fine features.

Raine stood, and slowly walked to the girl in the center of the room. Skye was staring at the floor in front of her, so still it was as if she were made of stone. Raine put her hands on the girl's shoulders.

"Skye," she said softly in the silent room, "I'm so sorry."

Skye muffled a sob and clutched Raine to her chest, and the Scinterian put her strong arms about her and stroked her hair. The assembly as a whole was baffled, and it was finally Talan who spoke to let them understand.

"Isleif is dead."

The pronouncement sent a gasp through the room. All in Arianthem knew of the magnificent wizard. He was as legendary as the dragons. Maeva moved to Skye, still not grasping the extent of the girl's loss and the depth of her grief. Granted, Isleif had always been bonded to the Tavinter, but...

"Isleif was Skye's great-grandfather," Raine explained, and Maeva drew back. This she had not known, and there were few things in Arianthem that escaped her notice. She put her hand on the girl's shoulder.

"I'm sorry, Skye," the Directorate said, and her condolences were heartfelt.

Skye pulled back from Raine and squared her shoulders, but the Ha'kan would not let her carry this burden alone or disappear into her reserve.

Queen Halla swept forward and pulled the girl into a motherly embrace, and the High Priestess was right behind her. The kindness and maternal love of the two was too much for Skye, and the tears again began to flow. The women held her while her shoulders shook with her silent grief. Raine felt the ache of grief in her own throat, as much for Skye as for herself.

The Queen and High Priestess escorted Skye from the room, followed by the First General and First Scholar. Several of the Tavinter were right behind them. Maeva was something at a loss as to how to proceed. It seemed inappropriate to continue the celebration, and the mood was certainly broken. The room was deathly quiet.

Unexpectedly, it was Idonea who stood to speak upon this solemn occasion.

"I have spent the last twenty years with Isleif," she began. "He was my Master, my teacher, and my friend. He was, without a doubt, the greatest wizard this world has ever known. He was capable of the most sublime magic I've ever seen and understood the arcane in ways that are unimaginable."

The assembly all nodded somberly.

"But if there's one thing I know about that old lecher," Idonea continued, startling the group with the blunt descriptor, "he wouldn't want us to sit around moping about his demise. He would want us to celebrate his life with the same zest and zeal he approached all things." She raised her wineglass to the room at large.

"To Isleif," she said, and the room responded in unison.

"To Isleif!"

The hum of conversation renewed, and although the mood was not as light-hearted as it had been at the beginning of the day, it did not devolve into a funeral.

"Thank you," Maeva said to Idonea. She was truly grateful for the mage's words and their result.

"You're welcome," Idonea said, as if it were no matter. But as the Directorate walked off, Talan saw the depths of grief her daughter had suppressed to give that speech. She stood and pulled the girl to her.

"Come here, my love," Talan said, and Idonea collapsed into her arms.

Raine sat down heavily, feeling Skye's grief, Idonea's grief, and her own. She had known the wizard almost his entire life, well over a hundred years. And although she hadn't known him well at first, the last few decades she had known him very well. Feyden brought her a glass of the chilled white wine he was fond of, and she took it with thanks. He sat down next to her, and they were soon joined by Lorifal. It was not long before both Dagna and Elyara made their way over, and all sat with Idonea as she retook her seat. The small group sat comfortably, talking quietly, and sipping their drinks. Talan leaned against the wall behind them in shadow, a watchful, calming sentinel.

A slow awareness began to come over the assembly as they watched the small group talk quietly amongst themselves. There was a bond between them, a camaraderie that went beyond mere friendship, even beyond romantic love. And smiles began to cross faces as they remembered or even realized for the first time who sat before them. The Emperor was slow on the uptake, not understanding the feeling of admiration that was taking hold in the great hall. Maeva saw the lack of comprehension on his face and spoke to him.

"You know who that is, don't you?"

"What are you talking about?"

Maeva nodded to the band, proud that her brother was counted in their ranks. "Two are missing, but that's the group, the six of them and the dragon, that traveled through the Veil over two decades ago and closed the Gates of the Underworld. They stopped an invasion in its tracks. And a few days ago, most of them fought in another battle to turn the Hyr'rok'kin back. That is a group of heroes, the like of which, this world may never see again."

CHAPTER 14

The sun rose as it always did, indifferent to the griefs and pains of mortals. It was not a cruel indifference, rather a patient one, an encouraging one, a sign that today could always be a better day.

It could. But today was not that day.

"What is that?"

Talan came out on the balcony to stand with Raine, drawn by the tone of her voice. Her eyes squinted, looking far across the land from the heights of Mount Alfheim. It was in the vicinity of the Empty Land.

"I don't know," Talan said, her concern matching Raine's.

It was a black cloud, possibly from a fire. But there was nothing to burn in the Empty Land. It looked something like a storm, but unlike any storm they had ever seen. And it looked like a cloud of dust, but too big for any natural source. The very fact that they could see it from that great distance was ominous.

"What is that?" Skye asked, coming out onto the shared balcony.

"We don't know," Raine said.

Senta, Gimle, and then the Queen joined them, with Astrid not far behind.

"Is that a storm?" Gimle asked.

"Not exactly," Talan said, her certainty growing as to the cause.

Soon, others were coming out onto adjacent balconies to witness the strange phenomenon. Maeva joined them on their terrace, followed by a host of others. Most were confused and frightened, but the group of heroes from the night before merely looked grim.

"Skye," Senta said, grabbing her arm. "Isn't that one of your signals?"

"Yes," Skye said in confusion. There shouldn't be any signals close enough for her to see. The Tavinter scout would have to pass into Alfar territory and set up a makeshift station in the forest for her to see it here.

"Wait a minute," Senta said, then ran into her suite. She returned bearing the ornate, full-length floor mirror from the vanity area. It had a pivot at its center, which Skye examined. She glanced up at the angle of the sun and the angle of the scout who was sending a request for acknowledgement at regular intervals.

"I'll need one more."

Senta ran into Raine's suite and returned with another mirror nearly identical. All watched with interest, albeit with little understanding. Senta leaned over to Maeva.

"The Tavinter have a way of communicating over long distances. It involves flashes of light of changing duration and frequency. It's how they stay in touch even though they're so few and spread across all of Arianthem."

"Amazing," Maeva said. And she thought her network was good.

"Perfect," Skye said, placing the mirrors so the light was directed back at the scout. She signaled to him that she was ready.

All watched with bated breath as the Tavinter concentrated on the flashes of light that meant nothing to them, but a great deal to her.

"There's an enormous force of Hyr'rok'kin massing in the Empty Land," Skye said, reading the signal.

"How many?" Raine asked.

Skye signaled the query, then paused at the reply. She requested confirmation, and the reply was the same.

"Hundreds of thousands."

There were gasps throughout and Talan looked to Raine. "These are numbers from the Great War."

"The recent battle was just a feint, then," Raine said, "a test of our capabilities. How far have they progressed into the Empty Land?"

Skye dutifully relayed the question and interpreted the response.

"Not far. They seem to be staging."

"So, there will be even more," Talan said. "I must go find Kylan, and rally my kind."

"Wait," Raine said, "here's another messenger."

A great hawk swept down from the sky, landing on the bannister of the balcony. It was so large that Raine had to look up at the bird when perched in such a way. All were astonished at the great bird, and even more astonished when Raine began to listen intently to the chirps and whistles, flutters and flaps of the creature. It communicated almost as much through body language as it did through sound, and Raine understood it completely. When the conversation was finished, her expression was even grimmer.

"She has seen the army up close, and it's a full-scale invasion. Horde Shards, Flying Shards, Marrow Shards, Reaper Shards, Hell Hounds," she paled slightly and stopped, which filled those around her with trepidation. Little fazed the Scinterian, so this had to be bad.

"What?" Talan asked.

"She saw a manifestation of the Membrane, the largest she's ever seen."

Talan carefully controlled her reaction, knowing that all present would follow their lead. Raine also gathered herself.

"What is the Membrane?" Maeva asked. It was her brother who responded.

"It's a terrible creature," he said. "We saw it in the Veil. It can destroy with a touch."

"And destruction is more desirable than what else it can do to you," Idonea added.

Raine's voice was calm once more, matter of fact. "There are also a number of those catapults, which will endanger all the dragons."

The Emperor was fairly in a panic. His land would be the first to fall to the invading horde. He knew he should be doing or saying something, but his mind was frozen with fear. Raine took one look at him and turned to Nerthus.

"What will Bristol do?"

"He'll begin moving the army into place along the edge of the Empty Land, most likely near where we battled before. It's the area of imperial territory that dips farthest into the desert, and it would be his objective to stop them there before they reach any towns or cities."

"How many troops?"

"He can deploy eighty thousand immediately. If he has two days, he can get close to two hundred thousand there."

Skye began signaling her scout once more, then carefully watched the response.

"The imperials are already staging," Skye said, "and where you estimate, Nerthus."

Raine was grateful for the presence of the very competent Knight Commander, and grateful that her comrade, Bristol, had remained behind.

"And the wood elves," Skye continued, "are already there, perhaps twenty thousand of them."

Elyara clasped her hands. It would be like Y'arren to send her people to stand against such an abomination. Raine nodded her respect and thanks to the slender elf.

"The Ha'kan can provide close to a hundred thousand troops," Senta said, "but it's a several day march from our land."

The Emperor was incredulous that the Ha'kan would respond to the aid of the empire. He thought for sure they would stage at their own border and make a stand there, regardless of treaties. It is what he would have done.

"Wait," Skye said, signaling her scout. It made sense that the same messages would have been relayed to Haldis, and that they would have gotten it sooner. She was right, and despite the grim situation, she smiled.

"The Ha'kan already know of the invasion, and Dallan leads the army forward. They're already near the imperial border."

"Good girl," Senta said under breath, and Halla's heart swelled with pride.

"The Alfar can provide eighty thousand of our finest," Maeva said, "and we can be there in two days' time."

The Emperor was again astonished at the selfless actions of the allies. The Alfar occupied a strategic position high in the mountains and could likely repel any invasion, or at least weather an extended siege from such favorable terrain. And yet they would ride forth into imperial territory, exposed, to come to the aid of others.

"Lorifal," Raine said, "can your people travel—," she paused, "in their usual way and get to the staging ground?"

Lorifal knew exactly what she was talking about and appreciated her discretion in front of the imperials. The dwarves considered all land underground to be theirs, and had tunneled extensively throughout imperial territories, despite the many treaties they had signed saying they wouldn't. They could travel for miles without ever coming to the surface.

"Aye lass, that we can. Fifty thousand of the finest warriors you'll ever see. I need only get word to them."

"Skye, can you send word to your scout for Lorifal?"

Skye nodded and the dwarf joined her as they quietly discussed the message the Tavinter would send to the dwarves.

"It seems we have a little time," Raine said to Talan. "You should go and rally your kind. I'll leave now with Drakar."

It was not a quarter of an hour before Raine stood with Talan on the terrace where they had arrived but a few days before. Drakar stood a respectful distance away, and a throng of people beyond him. Raine stood with a heavy heart, and Talan was inordinately stiff as both tried to present a composed departure for those watching. They embraced, briefly kissed, then Talan turned to leave.

"Weynild."

The name stopped the dragon in her tracks, and it caught Idonea's attention. It was a name that only Raine used, the one she had known Talan by first. And it was a name that Raine only spoke in intimate moments, primarily when they were alone or with family. It was an endearment, and to Idonea, it was a terrible omen.

The dragon turned around and crushed the Scinterian in an embrace, kissing her deeply, passionately, with an anguish that Idonea had not seen in her since Raine had set out on that quest so many years ago. And Raine's eyes were closed as she clutched her lover and pressed against her, but when they opened, they were the color of lavender in the fields. Talan took two steps away, her hand still holding the one that clung to her, then they released one another and Raine turned away. With extraordinary resolve, Raine willed the color of her eyes to change, the blue and gold marks rose on her forearms, her biceps, her shoulders, and her back. And when she turned around, she gazed at the dragon with clear eyes and a steadfast determination.

Talan disappeared into a flash of yellow light so brilliant it blinded all present. But Raine stared into the light, enjoying the pain it caused her. The fiery red dragon appeared, then roared as it leaped skyward. It climbed with rapidity, then wheeled about to turn eastward. It grew smaller and smaller as the Queen of all Dragons went to rouse her kind from their sleep.

"I know the dragons will rally to my mother's side much more than mine," Drakar said, "but I'm surprised she would part with you."

"We'll be together again on the battlefield," Raine said, "and she can always reach me if I need her."

"Right," Drakar said, "so shall we head south?"

The imperial troops watched fearfully as the black dragon appeared from the north, but it was the sharp-eyed wood elves who told them they had nothing to fear. The dragon circled once, then landed in an empty spot of the desert. A figure slid from his back, the dragon transformed, and then the two approached. Once Bristol could make out the identity of the dragon rider, he fairly ran to her.

"Raine!" he exclaimed, never so happy to see anyone in his life.

"Bristol!" Raine said, clapping him on the shoulder.

"I was getting a little nervous there," Drakar said, "I thought your archers were going to open fire."

"Bristol," Raine said, "this is Talan's son, Drakar."

Bristol shook Drakar's hand. "My apologies for that," he replied, "the troops are a little edgy. A group of dragons flew overhead not too long ago, heading in the direction of the Hyr'rok'kin. They appear to have joined them."

"Was one of them gold?" Drakar asked.

"Yes."

"It figures that bitch would turn up," Drakar said, "I'm going to enjoy killing her."

"The gold one is called Volva," Raine explained, "she's one of the last remaining Ancient Dragons, one that stood against Talan in the Great War."

"And now she will again, in the Second Great War."

Bristol's forbidding title indicated he knew how significant this war would be.

"My mother won't make the mistake of letting any of them live this time," Drakar said.

Another man approached and Raine was happy to see it was someone else she knew.

"Torsten!"

The Tavinter scout hugged Raine, ecstatic to see her.

"Skye's not far behind me," Raine promised. "I only beat her because I came by dragon."

"And the Ha'kan are not far behind me," Torsten said.

This was news to Bristol, and he didn't recognize this man who had just arrived. Raine stepped in.

"Bristol, this is the serving First Ranger of the Ha'kan—"

"—until Skye gets here," Torsten interjected.

"—and second in command of the Tavinter people."

Bristol appreciated the man's loyalty. "Well met," he said, clasping the man's forearm.

"The Ha'kan have been riding like the Valkyries," Torsten said, "led by their Princess. They're but a few hours away."

This was glorious news to Bristol. He had greeted the arrival of the wood elves with enormous relief and thankfulness.

"And nearly all the Tavinter are converging on this spot," Torsten added.

"Wonderful," Bristol responded.

"The Alfar are also on the way, eighty thousand strong." Raine said, "And the dwarves as well."

Bristol could not believe these reinforcements. He had looked across at the growing army and it filled him with dread.

"Some of the dwarves are already here," Bristol said. "'Tis strange, they appear out of nowhere."

"Yes...strange." Raine said, drifting off, then changing the subject. "And Talan will bring the dragons loyal to her, so we'll offset the winged Hyr'rok'kin and their dragons."

"I heard of the bat-like creatures," Bristol said darkly, "and the catapult they used against the dragons. We'll have to figure out how to neutralize that. I brought some of the mages from the Mage Academy. They are nothing like Idonea or Elyara, but they're considerably stronger since Idonea's intervention."

"Idonea and Elyara travel with the Alfar. They'll be here soon, as well."

"Do you think everyone will get here in time?" Torsten asked.

Both Bristol and Raine looked across the sparse landscape of the Empty Land, to the cloud and black dot at its far end. The fact that they could see it at all was a testament to its massive size.

"They'll rest, for it's not an easy climb up from the Veil. The Reapers and other wraith-like creatures can simply manifest, but the flesh-and-blood Hyr'rok'kin must hike. It's not an easy march across the Empty Land, either," Raine said.

"It took us several days," Bristol added, "and we were but a small band."

"We were lucky to get this much warning," Raine said, "this most recent army was almost upon us before we saw them, and we had but a few hours."

"I'm guessing it was more than luck," Bristol said shrewdly, "given that you left sentries behind after your last battle."

"I might have left a few watching," Raine said, "and I'm guessing Skye did the same thing given that the Tavinter knew so quickly."

"She relayed instructions that we were to watch this area day and night," Torsten confirmed.

"That sounds like her."

"So, everyone is coming," Bristol said, still unable to grasp the alliance that Raine had formed. "The elves, the dwarves, the Ha'kan, the Tavinter, all coming to fight on imperial soil."

"This is a battle for Arianthem," Raine said. "It rises above states and territories. We don't have an army of Scinterians this time, and the dragons are far fewer in number. But we're united as never before."

And for the first time since the cloud had appeared on the horizon, Bristol felt a ray of hope.

Raine stood watch, staring out over the desert, a solitary figure that many looked upon when they felt their courage falter. She stood for hours at a time, accepting the food and drink that was brought to her, but maintaining her vigil.

The Ha'kan forces were the first to arrive. They were magnificent, riding in on horseback, a wave of red and gold, the Ha'kan banners fluttering in the wind. The infantry marched behind, stretching as far as the eye could see. Bristol was humbled at their rise to aid.

"Raine!" Dallan exclaimed, dismounting from her horse. Both she and Rika went straight to the warrior.

"Dallan, Rika," Raine said, clapping them both on the shoulders. "Thank Sjöfn you're here."

"'Tis true we worship the Goddess of Love," Rika said, "but today we'll call upon Tyr."

"A good idea," Raine said. The God of War would probably be more useful on this day.

"The Tavinter relayed word that Isleif is dead," Dallan said, "is Skye all right?"

"It's hard to say. She mourns him deeply, but that Tavinter reserve fell in place right away. I'm guessing she travels with your mother because otherwise she would already be here."

Dallan nodded. The Tavinter could move faster than anyone she had ever seen.

"Fortunately, the elves are swift as well," Raine continued, "and Maeva has sent a large force, possibly eighty thousand, no doubt under the command of Feyden."

Bristol approached and greeted the Ha'kan warriors with the same relief and humility he had greeted all of the responding aid. The sight of the Ha'kan army, led by the dashing Princess and her First General, had heartened the imperial troops. Rika surveyed the vast expanse of the imperial army with a practiced eye.

"You have almost two hundred thousand here, no?"

"That's about right," Bristol said, impressed with the woman's acumen. She was young, but she knew what she was doing.

"Where would you like us to stage?" Rika asked.

"I was thinking over here to the south, guarding our left flank. That way imperial forces can bear the brunt of a frontal assault since we're the most numerous. And the elves and dwarves can fall in to the north as they arrive, on our right flank."

For the first time, Rika and Dallan turned their attention to the massive force on the horizon. It was hard not to feel a coldness, even a trace of despair looking at the enormous army. Although both Dallan and Rika had been in battle, this enemy was different: these were Hyr'rok'kin, the awful, flesh-and-blood manifestation of the Underworld, the abominations that vomited into the mortal realm.

"We were envious when we heard we missed your last battle," Dallan said quietly. "It was a foolish envy."

Raine was silent for a moment, her ice-blue eyes reflective. "My father's people were not afraid of death. They welcomed every opportunity to cheat it. The only Scinterians they mourned were those who did not die in battle. They even had a phrase for death, 'ior'dann'aka,' which means 'the lover who will not be denied.'"

Raine turned to Dallan and Rika. "I already have one of those."

Both women slowly grinned. They would follow this warrior anywhere.

"They're moving," Raine said, turning to Bristol.

"What?" Bristol said.

"They've begun moving. Slowly, but they're beginning to advance."

"Will everyone get here in time?"

"I believe so. My only concern is the dragons. They're the swiftest, but they're also coming the farthest."

"We should compare resources," Bristol said to Dallan and Rika. "My command tent is over here."

The two Ha'kan left with the Knight Commander, and Raine returned to her solitary vigil, staring far across the desert.

The elves arrived in grand style, imposing in their green and gold armor, flying the banners of the Alfar Republic. They were accompanied by the Ha'kan Royal Staff. Dallan ran to greet her mother, then stopped herself short, as did Rika.

"Your Majesty," Dallan said formally. "I return the throne to its rightful leader."

Rika pressed her forearm to her armored breastplate. "First General," she said with the same formality, "I return the army to you."

A smile played about Halla's face. "We're honored to accept." She then hugged her daughter, and the First General clapped an arm on her future successor.

"Well done, you two," Senta said.

Dallan turned to Skye and crushed the young woman in an embrace before she held her at arm's length. "I'm so sorry, Skye."

"Thank you," Skye said simply, then turned her attention to the dark cloud on the horizon. "They're moving."

It was unsurprising that the keen-eyed Tavinter had seen what only Raine had perceived thus far.

"Yes. Raine said they're moving slowly, but they are moving."

Feyden dismounted and greeted his old comrade, Bristol.

"Bristol, this is Commander Ayen. He'll be leading the elven forces."

"Not you?" Bristol said.

"No," Feyden said, "I've no doubt my skills as a warrior, but he's a better general than I am. I'll leave him to the strategy of troop movements. I," he said nodding at the solitary figure standing watch, "will be fighting at that one's side."

"Understood," Bristol said. He turned to Lorifal.

"Most of your people are already here."

The Knight Commander was joined by Nerthus, who assumed command of half the imperial forces. He invited the Ha'kan Royal Staff and the dwarven and elven commanders to his tent where they further discussed resources. Torsten reunited with Skye, and the Tavinter had a heartfelt reunion with their beloved leader. Idonea, Dagna, Lorifal, and Elyara stood with Feyden, all watching the solitary figure.

"She's been standing like that for two days," a nearby soldier proffered.

"Let me go see what this is about," Idonea said, and began picking her way carefully across the harsh landscape.

"It's funny, isn't it," Dagna commented. "Idonea fairly despised Raine when we set out on that quest so many years ago, and now they're so close."

Idonea came up beside Raine, and Raine acknowledged her presence with a brief nod, then returned to her vigil. There was a tension about the Scinterian that Idonea had never seen before, a tightness in her posture, a conservation of movement that suggested she might snap in two if she moved too quickly. Her breathing was slow and even, but purposeful, measured, like the breath of someone laboring underneath an enormous weight.

"What?" Idonea said at last.

The silence stretched out and Idonea did not think Raine was going to respond.

"The hand of fate," Raine said, "I feel as if the hand of fate is reaching out and closing around me."

"You've always told me you would make your own fate."

These words had a pronounced effect on Raine. They provided succor, encouragement, reminded her who and what she was.

"Thank you," Raine said, truly grateful for the words. She hugged Idonea, then returned to her steely-eyed watch.

Idonea moved a short distance away to join Drakar, and her brother hugged her more chastely than he had in his entire life. They both watched Raine stand staring across the bleak landscape. Although the exchange had brought comfort to Raine, the words had done no such thing for Idonea.

The army was getting closer. The call to general assembly was sent forth, and all the armies obeyed. On the left flank were the Ha'kan, a hundred thousand strong. On the right flank were the elves and dwarves, a hundred and fifty thousand in all. And in the center were two hundred thousand imperial soldiers.

The Tavinter archers would target the flying Shards. The Ha'kan archers would target the lumbering Marrow Shards. The Alfar archers would target the Hyr'rok'kin foot soldiers, and the wood elves would target the Reapers and any other magical atrocities, for the woodland warriors bore an arsenal of enchanted weapons.

And at the front of this glorious army stood Raine. A short distance behind her stood Idonea, Elyara, Dagna, Lorifal, and Feyden. Soon, Idonea and Elyara would move back to where they could wield their magic out of harm's way. They had debated leading with Idonea's wave of sand but decided against it. It was a killing blow, effective because they had mounted a charge and slaughtered the fallen. But they did not want to wade into the midst of this enemy and possibly be surrounded, and given the size of the approaching army, that was very possible. Elyara could raise temporary barriers, but she could not raise walls sufficient to keep this army out.

Raine could see the Horde very well, now. Not enough to make out individuals, but enough to make out individual features of the army. She could see the outlines of the catapults, the slithery presence of the Reapers, the bulk and size of the Marrow Shards. She could see the bounding of a pack of Hell Hounds, straining against their leashes. By her calculations, just in terms of numbers, they were outmatched two, possibly three-to-one. There were more than a million Hyr'rok'kin approaching on the horizon.

Raine went through options in her head once more. Because of the numbers, she had outlined clear circumstances for an orderly retreat. The Ha'kan would head south, the imperials due east, and the elves and dwarves would disappear back into the Deep Woods. They would all continue to fight, falling back in planned, coordinated maneuvers. Splitting the forces would be dangerous, but Raine was betting the Hyr'rok'kin were not disciplined enough to maintain ranks in a perceived rout, and they would be easier to fight scattered. The elves and dwarves would have good cover, and the Tavinter were particularly good at laying traps in their wake, so the Ha'kan would be protected. The imperials would need help, and Raine would be their rear guard if retreat became necessary.

Her steel-blue eyes returned to the catapults. Retreat would not be the first option. Skye would try and take out as many of those as possible. This thought brought her head around and her gaze to the heavens once more, scanning the northeast for signs of the dragons. They still had not been seen, and that could be a real problem. Right now they had only Drakar. An enormous gold dragon flew leisurely over the Hyr'rok'kin troops, accompanied by several lesser dragons. Gimle thought she could protect the troops from their fire with her wards for a short time, and Idonea thought she could deal with some of the lesser dragons with her spells. But that would drain Idonea, and that still left Volva. Raine had spoken quietly with Skye about the possibility of needing her to clear a path to one of the catapults without destroying it. That way Raine could lead an assault squad, her, Feyden, Lorifal, and a handful of others, to capture the catapult and use it against the enemy dragons. Her eyes returned skyward. That is, if her love did not arrive soon.

The details of the Horde became visible. The dark blobs became distinct soldiers, the bouncing packs became individual Hell Hounds, the slithery vapors emerged as Reapers. These last were particularly horrifying for few had ever seen them, and their two-tone shrieks, one high and one low, became audible. Even from that distance they could see their fang-lined maws, gullets so deep they disappeared into the earth itself. The dumb, brutal faces of the Marrow Shards were evident, grinning with anticipation, drool running down their chests and dowsing the foot soldiers below. The army marched forward, yelling and screaming, howling and growling, screaming and shrieking.

Raine gave one last glance to the northeast sky, then turned to face her enemy. She raised her arm. The Queen and First General of the Ha'kan took a deep breath. The Knight Commanders of the Imperial Army tensed. The elven and dwarven commanders steeled themselves.

And the army of Hyr'rok'kin stopped.

Raine's arm hovered in the air. Not only did the Hyr'rok'kin stop, they grew silent. The screams and shrieks ceased. The creaking of the catapults went quiet. The Hell Hounds sat down on their haunches. Even the dragons landed with a distant thud.

"What are they waiting for?" Feyden murmured.

Raine slowly lowered her arm. She was cold. Colder than she had ever been before. She knew exactly what they were waiting for.

The ground in front of Raine began to shift, shake, turn black as a vortex swirled upward from the earth. The vortex twisted, then writhed into a form. The form solidified into black robes, a black crown, and black eyes that transformed into glittering emeralds with a pupil that was slit like a snake, then resolved into normalcy.

But there was nothing normal about the woman who stood before Raine, dwarfing her. She was gorgeous: blood-red lips, startling green eyes, sharp cheekbones, a voluptuous figure that the robes did nothing to hide. Her expression was icy and volcanic, possessing ice and fire that would freeze or burn any mortal so foolish as to touch her. She gazed at Raine with desire, ownership, and victory.

"Hello, my love," the Goddess of the Underworld said.

The sarcasm in the voice was pronounced as Raine fought to keep from shivering. Her body always responded to evil by growing cold, and right now she was freezing. The blue and gold scars on her body were livid as if they strained to rip themselves from her skin. She took an inadvertent step back, which told her somewhere in the back of her mind that Hel was not yet restraining her: she still could move. Very slowly and deliberately, Hel extended the scepter she held and traced an oval in the air next to her. A glowing, burning portal opened.

Raine sought to keep her teeth from chattering. "You cannot take me from the mortal realm."

"Ah, and that has been your mistake all along," Hel said. She cast a significant glance at the portal.

The sounds of a horrific struggle emanated from the portal, as if some poor creature were in a fight for its very life. There were cries of pain, the clamor of thrashing, and the thud of blunt force on flesh. Demons shrieked and screamed, but Raine could not yet make out what hapless victim was under attack.

Hel casually continued her conversation, her malice palpable. "You see, you were under the impression that it was *you* I wanted all this time."

Raine stared at the portal in growing comprehension and horror. The tempo of the struggle was increasing, and the cry of the injured creature rang out. The cry was followed by a roar of pain from the desperately fighting creature. The Goddess confirmed Raine's rising understanding as her green eyes glittered.

"When it was Talan I wanted all along."

"No!" Raine cried. She took a step forward and stopped herself. Her hands went to the swords on her back, twirling them with a snap to the ready position. She stood, poised with indecision, straining to hear the struggle.

The Goddess was nonchalant. "I knew that Talan was using that bracelet to pass through Nifelheim. And I knew if I threatened you, she would again try to come to your aid." Hel's eyes gleamed. "This time, I was waiting for her."

Another cry of anguished pain split the air, and it was too much for Raine. She took two steps forward and dived headfirst through the portal.

"Raine!" Skye screamed. Dallan and Rika barely caught her before she ran forward.

"So predictable," Hel said with a sigh, closing the portal with a wave of her hand.

"You cannot take them from the mortal realm!" Skye screamed at the Goddess. "You cannot take them from the mortal realm!" She fought to free herself while Dallan tried to hold onto her for her own safety. She feared Hel would strike Skye down.

The Goddess was only amused, however, and responded to the girl's accusation. "But that's just it, I didn't 'take' them anywhere. Talan was trespassing in my domain, and Raine, well you just saw Raine. She entered my realm of her own free will."

Skye still struggled wildly, now sobbing with grief and rage. The Goddess was merciless in her indifference.

"Oh, and by the way, I lied." She smiled to herself, and it was not pleasant to see. "I wanted them both."

Skye collapsed to the ground, her shoulders heaving. No one else moved, too stunned to react. Hel turned and lifted her scepter to the Horde behind her, and to the shock of all present, the Hyr'rok'kin army wavered, shifted about, then turned on its heel. The flying Hyr'rok'kin winged around, the Reapers swayed back-and-forth, then winked away, the catapults were slowly wheeled about, the Marrow Shards changed their course, and as one, the enormous force began trudging back the way it came. Even the dragons took flight and headed north, away from the battlefield.

Hel's voice rang out across the remaining army. "People of Arianthem, heed my words. Go back to your lands, return to your families. The Empty Land is forbidden to you. Stay on this side of the desert, and you will never see the Hyr'rok'kin again. Disobey me, and I will unleash annihilation upon you." She raised her scepter. "Obey my words, and I will trouble you no more!"

She turned, dismissing them with her final, mocking words.

"I have what I came for."

CHAPTER 15

It was a stunned group that gathered in the imperial city. True to Hel's words, the Hyr'rok'kin marched back across the desert, disappearing into a shimmering haze of dust. The army of allies had little reason to remain; the battle was over before it had begun. No one had any idea how to proceed. The commanders of the respective armies sent their troops on a slow march in the direction of home, and the leaders agreed to meet in the closest of ruling cities, the imperial capital.

And so, it was a distinguished group that gathered in the Grand Hall of the imperial castle. Although not as stately as that in the Ha'kan palace, the room was royal, imposing, perhaps even a trace ostentatious. The painted visages of those who had previously sat on the imperial throne stared down at them. The empire did not have the lengthy history of the other races, but everything they had was thrown together in this room.

The room was not laid out as communally as the Ha'kan hall, either, and an unfortunate status was imposed upon the seating arrangements. Therefore, most chose to stand rather than sit in some disadvantageous position. Almost everyone milled about, hostage to the disjointed grief and shock which still pervaded their minds and mood. The Queen of the Ha'kan stood surrounded by the Royal Staff. The Imperial Knight Commanders flanked the Emperor, staring at the floor in front of them. Maeva stood with her assistants and Alfar military leaders. A group of very surly dwarves, all still heavily armored, stood off in the corner. Drakar stood leaning against the wall, brooding, his dark eyes filled with pain and anger.

But perhaps the greatest pain was centered in the room where Idonea stood, surrounded by Feyden, Lorifal, Dagna, and Elyara. Skye sat a short distance away, her head buried in her hands. Dallan hovered near her, still struggling with her own heartache, and anguished over her inability to console Skye. There were quiet murmurs of conversation, fits and starts as someone appeared just about to say something, then the room settled into quiet confusion once more. Finally, Skye could bear it no longer.

"I'm going after her," she announced, getting to her feet. "I don't care if I have to go by myself. Raine is still alive. I can feel her. And I'm going to find her."

The pronouncement was outlandish, ridiculous, but it served to cut through the fog that had settled on the group. Feyden spoke up, and at first, it seemed he was going to chastise her.

"That's probably not wise," he said. His tone changed. "If you go, you're going to need a guide, probably someone who's been there before." He glanced to his comrades, and Lorifal stepped forward, shifting his great axe.

"Aye lass, you're not going without us."

Skye looked to the heroes, and they all nodded as one. Her spirits started to lift, but then Queen Halla spoke.

"Skye, you're sworn to service of the Ha'kan."

The Queen sounded very stern and disapproving and Dallan clenched her jaw. A meaningful glance passed between the Queen and her First General.

"That's right," Senta said, stepping forward. "So, if you go, the Ha'kan must go with you."

Skye's heart swelled with gratitude, and Dallan's with pride.

"Feyden," Maeva said sharply, "you're my brother and my Second."

Feyden waited for his sister to give the order he feared he would have to disobey. But she, too, surprised him.

"So, where you go, the Alfar will follow. Even to the Gates of the Underworld."

The elven soldiers flanking Maeva struck their spears to their shields, an emphatic salute of agreement. The dwarves also raised their axes, indicating they would follow as well. To the Emperor, this was all spinning wildly out of control.

"What are you talking about?" he demanded, his voice shrill. "Are you insane?"

All eyes turned to him as he rose from his seat at the head of the table. "You heard the Goddess, she'll destroy us all!"

"And what would you have us do," Feyden shot back, "abandon Talan and Raine, who have sacrificed everything for this land?"

"I would," the Emperor declared, striking his fist on the table. "They have made the ultimate sacrifice. The Hyr'rok'kin have left our lands, the world can live in peace. It's a small price to pay for our safety. I will not endanger the lives of my people."

"You signed a treaty," Maeva reminded him. "You would abandon the Alliance?"

"What Alliance?" the Emperor said, "The Alliance is no longer needed, the war is over!"

"You have no honor," Maeva said, fairly spitting the words at him.

"Then we'll go ourselves," Queen Halla declared, "with or without imperial support."

"Then you'll bring disaster upon us all," the Emperor replied, "and I won't allow that. The only entrance to the Underworld is through the Empty Land, and the Empty Land is bordered on all sides by imperial territory."

The Queen was astonished, not only that this man would refuse to help, but that he might try to prevent them from taking action.

"You would forbid us passage into the Empty Land?"

"I would," the Emperor said firmly, "In fact, I would consider it an act of war if any nation passes through imperial territory to access the Empty Land."

Maeva was as incredulous as the Ha'kan Queen. "You would engage us in war at a time when we should all be fighting together?"

"Yes! Yes! I would! The Hyr'rok'kin are gone, and I would rather fight you than them!"

"That's a decision you may regret," Senta said coldly.

Nerthus and Bristol looked to one another. This was all falling apart because of the decisions of one man. They had both become soldiers while young, had lived their entire lives sworn to the duty of the Emperor, were bound by honor, tradition, and fealty to the empire, yet now they were faced with the most treasonous decision of their careers. They looked to one another, simply to decide which of them would make the move.

And were saved from doing so.

"You are as much a coward as your grandfather."

All eyes turned to the young woman who strolled through the double doors of the hall. She was slender, pale, lovely, and possessed an air of steel about her at odds with her waif-like appearance. Her carriage was noble, graceful, and her eyes glowed with a preternatural anger. She looked strangely familiar to Maeva.

"What is the meaning of this outrage?" the Emperor demanded. "What business do you have here?"

"I'm here to return the imperial throne to its rightful ruler."

"What?" the Emperor sputtered, fairly shaking with indignation. "And who in the world would that be?"

"Me," the young woman said calmly.

"Aesa."

The murmured name and recognition came from the lips of the elven leader. The Emperor's eyes drifted upwards to the likeness of his grandmother on the wall. The resemblance was striking, identical save for the dress. He dismissed the eerie similarity.

"That's impossible," he said, "my grandmother disappeared right after my father's birth, presumed murdered."

"Ah yes," Aesa said, casually moving through the rapt audience. "That was to be my fate. Slain by the assassin my husband sent to kill me."

"What?" the Emperor said shrilly. "How dare you make such an accusation!"

The Emperor's most-trusted advisor, for once shadowing someone other than him, stepped from Aesa's wake.

"She dares because it's all quite true. The contract is right here." And with that, the dark-robed figure unrolled an ancient scroll that looked terrifyingly official. The Emperor stared at the document as if it might bite him. "And that's my name," she pointed to the bottom, "right there."

And the Emperor stared at the one he thought was Malron'a, his advisor, his seer, his confidante. "And why is your name on there?"

"Because I was the assassin sent to kill her," the Head of the Shadow Guild said. She gave the Empress a sexually charged once-over. "And I did, sort of."

"You're a vampyre," Queen Halla said slowly.

"Yes," Aesa said, as if just coming to grips with that fact herself. "I am. But I don't believe there are any statutes that deny the throne based on vampyrism. Knight Commanders?"

Nerthus and Bristol again looked at one another.

"I don't believe there's anything in imperial law," Bristol said uncertainly, "disqualifying the undead from sitting on the throne."

"Good," Aesa said, "then remove that man."

Nerthus hesitated only a second, then directed her nearest soldiers to take custody of the Emperor.

"What are you doing? This is an outrage! I'll have you all beheaded..."

His voice trailed off as the former Emperor was dragged from the room. Aesa smoothed her skirts.

"Now, that little bit of unpleasantness is over. I reinstate all treaties with all peoples of the Alliance. The empire will honor its obligations to its allies." The empress grew quiet, even reflective. "I owe much to Raine."

Queen Halla was reminded of the recent conversation with Raine, where she had asked Halla if she remembered Aesa and spoke of a treasure dating from the dynasty of the House of Farlein. It was a wonder all the people that warrior had touched.

Aesa composed herself. "The path to the Empty Land is open, and the empire will cross that barren landscape with its allies!"

A great cheer went up in the room, and although little had been accomplished, it felt as if much had been done. There was a voice of reason to dowse a little cold water on that impression, a very ancient voice.

"Brave words from brave people," Y'arren said, "but how will you do this thing?"

The tiny, wizened matriarch was helped into the room by two robed acolytes, both wood elves. The old elf slowly made her way through the throng, supporting herself on her staff, and approached Skye. She stopped before her.

"Isleif told me to tell you goodbye. Your great-grandfather was very proud of you."

Skye felt a catch in her throat. She had successfully suppressed her grief through her bold call to action, as unreasonable as that call might have been. She did not want her grief to well up again.

"Why?" she asked, tears in her eyes. "Why did this happen? Couldn't Isleif see the future? Couldn't he have prevented this?"

"The future is never clear," Y'arren cautioned. "And even if he could see it, fate is very difficult to change. But his insight was very great, which is why he left you a gift. The one thing that you need the most right now."

Skye could think of many things that she needed; the list was endless. But what would her great-grandfather send to her? What would he anticipate she would need more than anything right now?

"What kind of gift?" Skye asked.

The ancient matriarch of the wood elves smiled, her eyes glowing with all the magic of the natural world.

"A plan."

EPILOGUE

That Scinterian had put up an incredible fight.

Hel looked down at the unconscious figure on the altar. The arms and legs were covered in blood and bruises. The armor was nearly ripped from her body, a fact that the Goddess appreciated because she could now see those beautiful muscles. She traced the bruises on the ribs, then the outlines of the abdominal muscles. Her fingers drifted down the armor to the opening on the thigh, then caressed the calf. She moved slowly around the foot of the altar, examining her captive, then began tracing the body up the other side. The muscled forearms were a wonder, the biceps so firm and round under such soft skin, the muscles robust even in unconsciousness.

Hel's gaze settled on the face, largely untouched even though the warrior had battled a legion of demons. There was a bruise on her temple, one the Goddess felt compelled to lean down and press her lips to. The features were chiseled, a strong chin, a straight, aristocratic nose, slightly full lips with a defined philtrum and small cupid's bow. Hel traced the lips with her fingertips.

Feray, her chief handmaiden, stood behind the Goddess as Hel continued her inspection of her prize. The handmaiden appeared older than Hel, wore similar but less elaborate robes, and bore a resemblance to the Goddess as all her handmaidens did: dark hair, dark eyes, lovely, but not as lovely as the Goddess herself. Faen, Hel's chief familiar, also hovered behind her, but while Feray waited patiently submissive, the demon hopped from side-to-side, something that would have irritated the Goddess had she not been so engrossed in her examination of her helpless prisoner. Each waited for their command.

"Feray," Hel said absently, "I give this one over to your charge."

Feray bowed as Faen grimaced his disappointment. He scuttled away.

"Of course, your Majesty. We will bathe and tend to her wounds."

"Hmm," the Goddess said, and turned to leave, her black robes swirling over the prone figure.

"What should we do with her when finished?" Feray called after her.

The five-word response implied the question was spurious, its answer self-evident. The hint of triumph implied the outcome had been inevitable.

"Put her in my bed."

ALSO BY SAMANTHA

Scan to see the series!

THE CHRONICLES OF ARIANTHEM

2nd CHRONICLES OF ARIANTHEM

THE DRAGON'S NIGHT (Book 9)
THE SCINTERIAN'S DREAM (Book 10)
THE RISE OF THE SINISTER (Book 11)

visit us on the web at

arianthem.com

follow us on Facebook

ABOUT THE AUTHOR

Samantha Sabian, author of the "Chronicles of Arianthem" series, enjoys writing about strong, sexy women. Not content simply to tell stories, she creates *worlds*. Her irreverent sense of humor often spills out of the mouths of her characters, who come alive in these remarkable fantasy settings.

Samantha lives in Southern California where she happily spends her day working out, attending art school, and of course, writing. She lives with a cacophony of parrots (more appropriate than "flock"), whose personalities find their way into her books, usually in the form of bossy little dragons.

Samantha tries to answer all email, so drop her a note:

Samantha@arianthem.com

www.ingramcontent.com/pod-product-compliance
Lightning Source LLC
Chambersburg PA
CBHW072052170626
46813CB00004B/1312